# Going Home

# Going Home

Cliff McNish

*Illustrated by Trish Phillips*

Orion
Children's Books

First published in Great Britain in 2014
by Orion Children's Books
a division of the Orion Publishing Group Ltd
Orion House
5 Upper St Martin's Lane
London WC2H 9EA
An Hachette UK company

1 3 5 7 9 10 8 6 4 2

A catalogue record for this book
is available from the British Library.

ISBN (Hardback) 978 1 4440 0629 2
ISBN (Paperback) 978 1 4440 1100 5

Printed and bound in Great Britain by
Clays Ltd, St Ives plc

People hand their dogs over to rescue centres for many reasons. Sometimes they move home and can't take a dog with them. Sometimes they can't afford to keep their dog any more. Sometimes the dog has severe behavioural problems, and when their owners have to give them up they're so upset that they weep their hearts out.

This book is dedicated to all those people who do their best to give homeless dogs a good life.

It is also for all the staff in organisations and charities who do so much to help homeless dogs. You guys are some of the most dedicated, professional and seriously underpaid heroes in the world.

And, finally, it is for Ciara McNish, whose happiest times in the last years of her life were spent with dogs, and whose story idea this was.

# Happy Paws

Happy Paws is the second biggest dog rescue charity in Gatesfield. Our eight large kennels house up to 120 dogs at any one time.

Click on the photos to view our wonderful, wonderful dogs!

Meet Fred, Happy Paws' oldest resident! Look at that smile!

### Foster Homes Needed
**Abandoned Puppies!**

Many lovely puppies find themselves unwanted due to irresponsible breeding. 6-month-old Cleo was found tied to a tree in Gurney Wood.

Read more >>

Rex, 2-year-old Scottish terrier. Desperately needs a kidney op.
Click his photo to find out more >>

## Dog of the Month: Ralph!

'Hi folks!
I'm Ralph.
Yes, I'm your Dog of the Month!
I hope that you're not put off by my crumpled face. I know that it's slightly scary, but actually I'm really nice.
I'm waiting in kennel five right now to say hello. Why not come and see me? I could be curled up on the carpet of your living room by supper time!'
Click here to find out more >>

*'Don't forget us cats!'*
We also have a small cattery at Happy Paws.
Click here to meet Olivia Darling Sparkle

**Sponsor a Happy Paws dog**

**Become a Happy Paws Pal**
Click here for details

Our dogs have to be neutered, vaccinated and microchipped. That's expensive!
All donations are welcome, no matter how small!

**Become a Happy Paws Pal**
Click here for details

# Happy Paws

***Ralph*** *– our wonderful Dog of the Month!*

## *Hi!*

My name is Vicky Masters (I'm the one stroking Ralph!) and I've been a kennel manager at Happy Paws for three years. In that time I've seen all sorts of fantastic dogs here, but I can honestly say I've never met a more loving companion than Ralph.

He's a wonderfully happy boy. There's always a wag in his tail, and he's incredibly gentle.

In fact, he's absolutely perfect!

Ralph's sad story is that he was discovered all alone in a house with his elderly owner, Muriel, lifeless beside him. Poor Muriel seems to have had a heart attack. By the time anyone found out there was a serious problem, several days had passed.

During all that time the amazing Ralph stayed by her side. He never stopped barking for help. We know this because, when our vet at Happy Paws examined him, he found that Ralph's throat was so badly damaged he could hardly make a sound. Even now, four years on, Ralph can only make little huffing barks.

I'm sure you will have noticed by now the terrible injuries to Ralph's face, but please don't be put off! He got them bravely saving a puppy that was being attacked by a much larger hound.

Ralph's such a great, great dog. He really is.

He loves his exercise, too, but he doesn't need to be exercised much. He likes nothing more than to put his head in your lap and have a little sleep while you stroke him.

He's clean, not at all destructive and gentle with children of all ages.

And if you have a cat, a rabbit, or some other small furry pet already, don't worry, because Ralph is good with them as well!

So what are you waiting for? Come and see him! Please bring beautiful, lovely Ralph into your life!

We're open every day to the public from 10.00 a.m. to 5.00 p.m. If you have any questions about Ralph or any of our other dogs, I'll be more than happy to answer them. Just call or email Happy Paws and ask for me

*Vicky Masters.*

# Chapter One

'Got a joke for you,' Mitch says. 'A beagle, a corgi and a cat are all stuck in a rescue home. One day the beagle bites on an empty plastic bottle in his cell, and out pops a genie.

'"You've got one wish," the genie says.

'"Wow," says the beagle. "Then I wanna be outta here!"

'The genie snaps his fingers and magics him out of the rescue home.

'Seeing this, the corgi runs up and bites the empty plastic bottle. Out pops the genie again.

"'One wish, remember," he says. "Don't waste it!"

"'Right," says the corgi, his tongue hanging out in excitement. "I want to get out of here, too. But I want a giant mountain of hot, fresh pork bones waiting for me as well."

"'OK," says the genie, and the corgi vanishes.

'The cat's been watching all of this. About an hour later she slinks up to the bottle and nips it with her claws.

"'One wish," says the genie. "Hurry up."

"'Well," purrs the cat, "I must admit I'm getting a bit lonely here in the rescue home all on my own. I think I'll have my two friends back."'

It's 8.00 a.m. and Mitch is awake.

And that means telling jokes and *fully* awake. As in bouncing around, whacking the walls awake.

'Farrgwa! Farrgwa! Gaddy! Gaddy! WEEEEEEE!' he yowls. It's his wake-up call every morning to all dogs in the world.

I've never met a dog with more energy. Or enthusiasm. Or sense of fun. He's been stuck at Happy Paws for three years and counting. Our fantastic kennel manager, Vicky, has managed to get him a new home eight separate times, but no one keeps Mitch for long. I'll tell you why later.

2

'Hrrrrrrrrrrmmm!' Mitch is running around his cell now, chasing his own tail.

Five seconds later he headbangs the bars dividing his cell from mine. Then has a good gnash on the metal.

'Grrrr! Yeaowwww!' he growls. 'That's better.'

Mitch is a moving, grooving rocket of non-stop energy. He also happens to be one of my two very best friends here at Happy Paws.

He's a brown and white Jack Russell terrier. A terrier with *attitude*.

My other great friend is in the cell to my left – the wonderful Bessie. She's a black and white border collie, and everyone lucky enough to meet her loves her.

Right now she's lying on her side, drenched in wintry dawn light. She's still asleep, and from the way her paws are twitching I think she must be dreaming. Sweet dreams, I hope.

The other dog still asleep – well, *snoring*, actually – is Fred. Fred hardly ever bothers to get up these days. He's an ancient white bulldog. A big, grouchy fellow. A heavy breather as well. And a slobberer. Not that he can help that. All bulldogs are slobberers.

'Wake up, cheerful!' Mitch calls across the kennel to him.

Fred stiffens his tail and gives a grouchy snort from his corner cell.

'Hey, I'm talking to you!' Mitch yells. 'Or are you gonna sleep all week again?'

'Shut up,' Fred blurts, not even opening his eyes.

'Dribbler!' Mitch barks back.

'Cat-brain!' Fred snarls, reluctantly waking.

To be honest, I sometimes think that squabbling with Mitch is the only thing that gets Fred up at all these days. I think he's given up hope of ever getting out of Happy Paws. He was dumped here eight years ago. That makes him Happy Paws' oldest resident. No wonder he just lies there miserably, hardly moving.

Not that Mitch, Bessie and I are much better off. Bessie's been stuck here for two-and-a-half years. Mitch for three. Me for four. When I tell you that most of the dogs taken in by Happy Paws find new homes within a couple of months, you'll realise that we have big, BIG problems.

In fact, unofficially, most of the staff call Mitch, Bessie, Fred and me the 'No-Hopers'. As in *there's no hope of them ever getting out of here.*

In my case . . . well, you must have seen my picture by now. Be honest: if you visited Happy Paws, with around one hundred and twenty dogs to choose from, would you really take home a dog that looked like me?

Not that I was born like this. I was less than a year old when a huge mastiff hound attacked me, badly damaging the whole left side of my head.

'Best give up hope, Ralph,' Fred told me recently. 'If anyone was going to take a dog with a face like yours

4

home with them, they'd have done it by now. There'll always be healthier, better-looking dogs than you. Stop trying. Life in here is easier that way. Sleep and eat. It's enough.'

And on my bad days I think maybe Fred's right. Even making me 'Dog of the Month' on the website hasn't made much difference. So far there's only been one enquiry about me. It came from a photography student who thought my head looked 'interestingly wrecked and cool'. He wanted to take some close-up shots. 'For my college project,' he said to Vicky. 'Ralph's ruined face will look great when I blow it up to poster-size.'

Vicky – who *never* gives up hope for us – kicked him out.

But after the student left Fred growled, 'There you go, Ralph. The only person interested in you is someone who wants to show you off as a freak for all to see. Your injuries are just too hideous. When will you finally accept that you're never going home?'

*Going home.*

It's what the Happy Paws staff call it when one of the dogs leaves here with a new owner.

'Patch is going home,' they'll say.

'What happened to Sammy?' A big beaming smile, followed by, 'He's gone home.'

It's what all of us dogs at Happy Paws dream about – the chance to go home. The chance to live in a proper house again. To walk off-lead. To sleep on a carpet, instead of a stone floor. To lie beside a fire. Simple things like that.

That's not too much to ask, is it?

And I refuse to accept that it'll never happen to me. I won't listen to Fred. I know I look horrible, but I could still get out of here, couldn't I? Someone *might* want me. Call me stupid, but anything's possible in this world, isn't it?

Whatever happens, anything's better than becoming like Fred, curled up despondently at the back of his cell refusing to look at visitors any more.

'Come on, we just need to try even harder to get people's attention,' Bessie said, giving Mitch and me a pep talk at the start of the year. 'Be even friendlier to visitors. Wag our tails till they fall off if we have to. Make a special effort to get noticed.'

And she's right.

Which is why this morning I'm practising my backflip.

It's an incredible trick an ex-circus whippet called Wally showed me. A reverse somersault. You go up and over backwards, landing again on all fours. I've been trying my hardest for weeks to master it – anything to distract people from my face. The trouble is, I keep falling on my head.

'Ouch!' Mitch winces, as he watches me land with another crunch on my chin.

Then, seeing I'm not hurt, he giggles, chases his tail and barks his head off for a couple of minutes. When he's finished screaming 'Waaaaaa!' for the fifth time he stops as suddenly as he started, sits on his haunches and says, 'Did I ever tell you about a Rottweiler I knew once called Fifi Woowoo?'

'Unfortunate name for a big dog,' I say.

'I know. Her owner liked tying pink bows around her neck. Put a pink hat around her ears, too. Painted her nails pink. Made her wear a pink leather jacket with "Hot Dog, I'm so gorgeous" written on it.'

'What happened to her?'

'She ended up being taken to dancing lessons for years. Puppy jive.'

As I grin, a new voice cuts through the kennel.

'Hello, boys.'

A quiet voice. Gentle and amused.

Bessie.

'Ah, the beauty awakens,' Mitch says, wagging his tail.

We watch as Bessie straightens out her hind legs and gives her spine a big leisurely s-t-r-e-t-c-h. The way Bessie does it – with a little shiver and a chuff of pleasure – you'd think that simple leg stretch she does every morning is the most exciting thing in the world.

Bessie's lovely. A pure-bred border collie with black and white patches, her fur is so glossy that even in this place she shines. She's smart, too. Did you know that border collies are the smartest dog breed in the world? It's true. They're smarter than Alsatians, smarter than Dobermans, smarter than all the rest of us. While that makes a lot of collies irritable if they get stuck in rescue centres like Happy Paws, Bessie isn't like that. She's incredibly warm and friendly – at least to other dogs. She even tolerates Fred, which requires a saintly level of patience.

'Mm,' she says, once she has Mitch's attention. 'What's this I hear about you picking an unnecessary fight yesterday?'

'Me?' Mitch answers, all innocence. 'Moi? Mr Nice Guy? Wouldn't harm a kitten, me.'

'That's not what I heard,' Bessie says. 'I heard you nipped the legs of a Belgian poodle.'

'Bessie, you're way off the mark there,' Mitch insists, laughing. 'I was only trying to get him to play. Wagging my tail non-stop, I was, saying *bonjour, bonjour*. Couldn't have been friendlier. I was just jumping on him, that's all. A bit of fun. He misunderstood. You know what poodles are like – so sensitive. He decided to turn it into a little scrap.' Mitch grins. 'Even that was fun. He *loved* it. Only titchy nips of his poodly tail. No harm done.'

'Titchy nips of his poodly tail . . .' Fred shakes his head. 'You nutter.'

Grinning, Mitch lets his tongue flop out like a dizzy

8

puppy. 'Oh,' he says, 'I so love you, stinky uncle Freddy.'

Bessie sighs, and is about to say something else when – fumble, fumble, key in the lock – Sloppy Steve makes his entrance.

# Chapter Two

The lights snap on.

Phew! Light.

After fourteen dark hours with only street lamps shining through our window we all bark excitedly.

Sloppy Steve – ten minutes late as usual – staggers into kennel five.

It's hard to describe Steve without sounding mean, and I'm not even going to try. He's a lanky, lazy, moany twenty-five-year-old who never smells entirely clean – at least, not to our sensitive dog noses.

Most of the kennel hands here at Happy Paws adore the dogs. Since it's a charity and they get paid next to nothing, love's the only reason they're here at all. But working with us just seems to be a job to Steve, and not one he likes much.

The first thing he does is *sit down*. That's Sloppy Steve's main activity – resting. The only reason he comes in on the early shift is to get half an hour to himself, doing nothing, before anyone else arrives.

After his first rest, with a groan he gets out the kennel mop, squishes it in a bucket with disinfectant and begins slopping out our cells. You might think that's why we call Steve 'Sloppy'. It's not. We call him that because he does everything so *half-heartedly*. Basically, Steve's rule of life is 'take it easy'.

He regards anything he has to actually *do* as hassle.

Mess on the kennel floor – hassle.

A dog doesn't look very well when he first arrives – double hassle. Why? Because he'll have to check the dog and, if it's ill, call our vet, T-bone, to take a look.

He doesn't like it when we make any noise, either. Dogs barking – hassle. Dogs barking because *they need their breakfast, because he's kept them waiting for it* – more hassle.

'Oy, we're hungry!' Mitch barks at him, but he might as well not bother. Sloppy Steve is impossible to hurry.

'Hey, you, speedy!' I yap, adding to Mitch's barks.

'Duhghhhh?' Sloppy Steve fractionally turns his head. Gapes like a fish. Then he leaves his mop on the

11

floor and collapses like a dying man into his padded red chair. Steve loves his red chair. Nearly all the stuffing's been knocked out of the cushions from the endless number of times he's slumped into it.

For the next fifteen minutes he does nothing at all except stare at the walls. Finally he runs his hands through his lank brown hair and reads the instruction notes left for him by Vicky last night. Whatever he reads makes him groan and curse.

'Now look at that,' Bessie says, grinning. 'Steve's grumpy and disappointed. Which means he's been given extra work today. Which means . . .'

'NEW DOG!' Mitch and I yell together.

Sure enough, Sloppy Steve staggers moodily across to the kennel notice board, picks up a thick red marker pen and writes . . .

## 2 NEW DOGS – Cleo and Ravi.

Once you've seen enough written words they aren't that hard to read and all of us, except Fred, stare at the board, blinking with interest.

New dogs add a bit of colour to the day. There are always more dogs than places available for them at Happy Paws, and usually our kennel is as full as the others. Two retrievers went home yesterday, though, so we've got a couple of spaces available.

For Sloppy Steve the arrival of any new dog is a

12

nightmare. It means putting fresh water down. It means getting out the special welcome treats. It means extra paperwork. All hassle, when he could be sitting on his backside reading his paper or playing games on his mobile.

'Ravi sounds like a street dog name to me,' Mitch decides. 'They're called names like that, aren't they? Ravi. Revi. Ravioli.' He starts laughing. 'Cleo. Cleggo. Leggo! Leaaaaaaaaaaaaa!' And he's off again, chasing his tail.

Not that he can chase it far. Kennel five is by far the smallest at Happy Paws. It's just an old converted storage area. We dogs each get our own room, or 'cell' as they call them, but the narrow walkway running down the middle of the kennel between the six cells is barely wide enough for staff and visitors to pass each other.

Sloppy Steve finally remembers to feed us. *Blu-blu-blu*, we hear, as his bony fingers spoon the wet breakfast into our bowls.

What food will it be today? Unfortunately, we know only too well – Binky's. Three months ago, dog food manufacturer Binky gave Happy Paws seven free lorry-loads of food. That's great for Happy Paws – as a dog charity it's forever short of funds, and needs all the free food it can get – but the downside is that we dogs have to actually eat it.

Today it's Binky's 'fun-shaped chicken wobbly-chunks in rich smack-your-lips jelly sauce'. Which tastes exactly – and I mean *exactly* – like mushy leather dipped in slimy chewing gum.

We gulp it down anyway. You eat what you're given here. I'm personally fond of anything with duck in it. Mitch likes fish and dental sticks, but he wolfs down everything. Bessie's a beef girl, but she'll chew on pork willingly enough.

Fred's the fussiest of the lot of us. He'll go days without eating sometimes, which troubles Vicky no end. Actually, I'm convinced Fred does this deliberately just to make her worry about him. That's the kind of annoying dog he is.

'Oy, this tastes rubbish!' Mitch barks, and carries on barking until Sloppy Steve flicks him a tiny liver chew.

Big mistake.

We all bark then until we get one.

'You lot will be the death of me,' Steve whines, holding his head. 'I haven't even had me fag or me ham sandwich yet. Just give me some peace, yeah?' Which, since he's been stuffing his own face non-stop since he arrived, just makes us all laugh and bark more.

Even Fred joins in our food protest today. It's like a gun going off when he barks – huge, hollow booms – *HUF, HUF, HUF.*

'OMG, shut it, shut it, you're doing my head in, man,' Steve bleats, slamming his hands over his ears. 'You're making me go mental.'

'You all right there, are you, Steve?' a sharp cockney voice calls from the doorway.

It's Jens – short for Jennifer. Jens is our second kennel hand. She helps out Vicky and Sloppy Steve for a short shift in the morning and again early in the afternoon. The rest of the time she's in kennel three, the enclosure where they keep the puppies.

Jens is brilliant. She's about twenty-two and covered in these weird snake and butterfly tattoos. She's famous for her black lipstick. Her hair is black, too, and so spiked and lacquered up that it makes a crunching noise when it brushes against anything.

We all like Jens. Sloppy Steve's a bit scared of her, but only because she's always catching him asleep in his red chair and he worries she'll report him to Vicky.

'Hi! Mornin'!' he calls out, snatching up his cleaning mop and pretending to be hard at work.

Jens isn't fooled, though. She heads to the kennel desk and plugs in her iPhone. Within seconds she has a brew on and is swaying to the rhythm of a punchy song called 'Now I'm Feeling Zombified'.

'You were supposed to give Fred a vitamin supplement this morning,' she notes, checking all the handwritten charts hanging outside our cells. 'Have you done it?'

'Er . . . yeah,' Steve lies.

Jens gives him a withering look and does the job herself.

'All right, all right,' Steve moans, watching her grumpily. 'Can't a man have one single minute of peace?'

But suddenly – hey! – none of that matters, because it's 9.00 a.m. and, though Fred's tucked his tail away, pretending he doesn't care, I can see that even he's secretly wagging it underneath him as – *whoosh!* – the door bangs open and she's here.

Vicky.

# Chapter Three

'How are all my beautiful boys and girls doing, then?'

Vicky breezes in, her heels clacking across the stone kennel floor. As always, the first thing she does is unbolt the latch of my cell and pull the door wide.

'Ralphy!'

'Vicky!' I bark, leaping into her open arms. I'm a bit out of control, shoving my nose in her face and pawing her. I know how stupid it looks as she puts me down

17

and I jump all around her, licking her hands and yelping her name, but I can't help myself.

Vicky's twenty-three and pint-sized. Five foot one at most, with frizzy blonde hair and a fringe that's always falling into her eyes.

Kissing me on my wet nose, she swiftly opens up the cells of the other dogs.

'Hey, guys, one at a time!' she laughs as Mitch and Bessie jump all over her.

Vicky's in charge of everything in kennel five – our safety, our walks, what we eat, visits to T-bone, as well as dealing with visitors. It's a lot of responsibility, but she never complains. 'You're absolutely purrfect, Ralph,' she whispered in my ear the week she arrived. 'It's only a matter of time before we find you a new home. You just need a bit of luck, that's all. A great dog like you, it *will* happen, I promise. Don't give up, beautiful boy.'

*Beautiful boy.* That's what she always calls me. It's untrue, of course. It's the opposite of what I really am. But that's Vicky for you. She's a bit blind when it comes to the dogs she's responsible for.

Call me silly, but I think she has a special place in her heart for me as well. I know she loves all the other dogs in kennel five to bits, but deep down I like to think, well, that I'm the one she'd keep for herself if she could.

'I'd take you home with me today, Ralphy,' she

murmured tearfully to me only last year after the staff Christmas party. 'If it wasn't for Misty, I would. You know that. I'd take you home right now.'

Misty. I'm sick of hearing that name. She's a greyhound from Ireland that Vicky rescued years ago. A dog so badly abused she attacks anything that comes near her. There's no way I'm strong enough to stand up to her, and Vicky can't throw Misty out of her house as no one else would have her.

That's the kind of person Vicky is. She always takes on the hardest dogs.

It's why Bessie, Mitch, Fred and I are all in her kennel. No one else wants us.

Greeting Sloppy Steve and Jens, Vicky encourages us back into our cells and heads to what she jokingly calls her 'office'. It's tiny. Just a space with a couple of chairs and a little round table where she perches her laptop, the kettle, tea, coffee and cakes.

Once she's settled, she heads into Fred's cell and gives him a big old hug. Fred reacts by just lying there like a sack, pretending to be asleep. He always does that, but we dogs can tell he secretly enjoys it and I think Vicky can, too.

'He's depressed, that's all,' I overheard her whisper once to Jens. 'He's been here far too long to care any more. He's sick of trying to impress visitors, sick of his cell, sick of everything. I don't blame him for ignoring us.'

After spending a few minutes with him, Vicky fetches herself a tea, then grins at me. 'Guess what, Ralphy? It's your birthday!'

We all bark out a laugh. It's an old joke. Vicky always hangs a doggy birthday notice on the outside of the kennel door. She'll do anything to get us extra attention. Monday morning means it's my turn.

*DOG BIRTHDAY TODAY!*

*Ralph!!!*

*HUGE fresh cream cakes FREE for all customers!*

'Any chocolate ones today, then?' Steve asks.

Even though it's Vicky who buys the cakes every morning, Sloppy Steve's already drooling over them. He loves his cakes, our Steve does. The only time he ever looks truly happy is when he's stuffing the leftovers into his mouth at the end of his shift. It's amazing he's so thin.

It's as Vicky's answering him that – *ding, ding* – the clock strikes ten.

Which means . . .

'SHOWTIME!' Mitch yells.

Yep. Ten o'clock is when Happy Paws opens its doors – when us dogs become officially AVAILABLE TO VIEW BY THE PUBLIC.

'Here we go!' Mitch barks, instantly keyed up and raring to go. 'Come on!' He stares excitedly at the entrance door, already so wound up his eyes are almost popping out. 'Oh, boy!' He sniffs the air. 'Oh boy, oh my, here we go! Get ready. GET READY, Ralph! Get ready to RUMBLE!'

As always, he's ridiculously disappointed when no one immediately bursts into the kennel dying to take him home.

Weekday mornings are always quiet, but even at weekends – when the rest of Happy Paws is chock-full of visitors – kennel five, full of us No-Hopers, is always slow. We're by far the least visited kennel. We're on the third floor, at the top of the building. Visitors have normally seen more than enough other dogs before they ever get to us.

By 11.00 a.m., with still no one in sight, Mitch is going slightly insane. Jumping up at the ceiling, he tries to bite the light.

'What are you doing, Mitch?' Bessie sighs.

'YEEOOWSIE!' he growls. 'Come on, people! Visit us! Come on, come on, come on, come on, come on, COME ON!'

Sloppy Steve looks blissfully happy. With nothing to do, he can sit with his legs crossed, reading his paper.

As for Fred, he utters not one sound. He always goes quiet during visiting hours. Sleeps, mostly. Ignores everything.

21

'WAGFAAA! WAAAAAA!'

By 11.15 a.m. Mitch, yapping with frustration, has latched his teeth onto one of the bars of his cell and is swinging like a chimp from it. It's an impressive trick, but he's chipped a couple of teeth doing it over the years.

Vicky slips into the corridor. I hear her out there, waiting like a tarantula to pounce on anyone walking by our kennel. It's a classic Vicky tactic – drag them in if you have to.

Finally, she hauls a man in to see us. He's wearing a T-shirt with a skull on it. He's a tough-faced guy, too. Not that Vicky's intimidated. He almost topples over as she yanks him inside.

'Me and my wife were just about to leave, actually,' he says grumpily. 'We have a bus to catch and what I'm really looking for is the puppies . . .'

'Ickle puppies!' all of us chant.

We always do that when anyone mentions puppies. Most of the people who come in our direction are looking for the pups in kennel three next door. We often have one or two of their spill-overs if the puppy enclosure is full, but not today.

'Ah, you want a *young* dog!' Vicky says brightly, the same thing she's said a thousand times before. 'Of course you do! And deciding between dogs is so *tiring*, isn't it?' She wraps her fingers like steel bolts around his bicep, dragging him towards us. 'So many of them

22

at Happy Paws, but how do you choose? I can see straight away that you're just looking for a nice family mutt. We have plenty of those . . .'

'Er, well, my wife's waiting for me and that,' the man says, his eyes hovering uncertainly over us.

But Vicky's already read the man right and slyly leads him towards Mitch.

'Ah, is that a Jack Russell?' the man asks.

'It is,' Vicky says. 'You obviously know your dogs. And Jack Russells make perfect family pets, of course.'

'Do they?'

'Oh, yes.'

Mitch is grinning now. 'Here we go!' he says, winking at me. 'Watch this, Ralphy-boy. I'll be out of here by lunchtime.'

Mitch isn't just bragging. Almost all the dogs at Happy Paws have their own way to grab a visitor's attention – an act, something unique to make them stand out from the crowd. But Mitch, clever boy that he is, has something extra.

He has what he calls THE PERFORMANCE.

Bessie smiles at me as we trot eagerly to the front of our cells to watch.

'Hello mister, hello mister.' With quick-fire waggles of his ears, Mitch starts with his usual leap from one side of the cell to the other.

The man's eyebrows rise.

'Yessiree!' Mitch yowls. 'You want me to carry the

23

morning newspaper to your bedroom? No problem. Rrrrrr.' Mitch is crossing the floor in dainty steps now. It mesmerises the man.

'Bring your slippers?' Mitch chirps. 'Fine. Whatever you like! WAAAAAAAAA!'

The man has no idea what Mitch is barking about, but he's curious. And now that Mitch has his attention he switches to his speciality – his amazing puppy impression.

'Ickle puppy! Ickle, ickle, ickle puuuppy,' he says in a tiny, melting voice.

The man smiles.

'Hold me up!' Mitch croons, going all wobbly-legged. 'I'm a puuuppy, too weak to stand! I can barely hold my head up, I'm so soft and droopy . . .' He's draping his tongue across his teeth now.

'Oh, he's a nice little fella, isn't he?' the man says, kneeling down in front of Mitch.

Mitch trips – seemingly accidentally – over his toes, goes cross-eyed, sighs, and somehow barks at the same time.

'Give him the whimper of need,' Bessie calls out. 'He's ready for it, Mitch. Give it to him!'

'Ooooh, look at me!' Mitch wriggles and – only he can do this – with a dreamy, floppy twist of his head, turns his face upside down and gives the man an irresistible puppy whimper.

'Perfect,' Bessie sighs, her mouth open in admiration.

The man is gobsmacked. The whimper of need has done it again.

'I'm so young and hopeless and *lovely*,' Mitch barks, batting his eyelashes. 'Oh, take me home with you. Take me home . . .'

In his cell, even Fred, trying not to, is laughing away. We all are. And who knows what might have happened next, except that the man suddenly spots the notice over Mitch's cell:

### 'Mitch is not suitable for those with cats.'

The man frowns. 'I'm afraid we have two pussy cats,' he says, looking genuinely disappointed. 'One of them is quite old and nervous, too.'

'Ah,' Vicky says, her shoulders slumping. 'That's a pity.'

And it really is because, there's no getting away from it, Mitch chases cats every chance he gets. It's only the usual friendly dog–cat rivalry. He's not interested in actually hurting them. With Mitch it's always just a mad, fun chase. But he keeps on ending up back here at Happy Paws because he simply *cannot stop doing it*.

The man – taking his chance to escape – mumbles his excuses and hurries off to kennel three.

Mitch watches him forlornly. 'Close,' he moans. 'That was *so* close, Ralph! Did you hear what he said? Not just one but two cats at his house to chase ! Like a dream come true . . .'

Half an hour later, we're tucking into a handful of Binky's tasteless 'oh-so-scrumptious bacon bites' when a long-faced woman with bulging eyes sticks her head around the door.

She's followed by an unhappy-looking man.

'We've already got three, Anita!' he's complaining. 'And these are the rubbish dogs no one wants.'

'Oh, shut up, Jerry,' she mutters. 'We'll just see what they're like.'

Vicky's eyes widen like saucers when she sees Anita. She's knows a dog-obsessive when she spots one. They've got a certain look. An unblinking, excited look. To the kennel managers at Happy Paws, people like Anita are like *gold dust*.

'Hello, it's a special occasion!' Vicky declares, giving them both the widest smile you ever saw. 'We've got lots of luxury cream cakes in honour of Ralph's birthday. There are far too many chocolate éclairs. You wouldn't help us eat them, would you?'

Not that Vicky needs to say anything to Anita. The woman is already ogling us.

'Mmm, chocolate,' she says absently, but she's not really listening. She heads like a laser beam straight for Fred's cell.

'Anita, we've got to go,' her husband, Jerry, groans.

'You promised we wouldn't get another dog. You promised! I knew when you steered the car this way you were going to drag me back here.'

'Chocolate éclair?' Vicky says sweetly to him, shoving one under his nose.

'I don't like éclairs,' Jerry says tetchily.

'We have almond croissants.'

'I don't like croissants, either.'

Fred is so lifeless in his cell that even a dog-lover like Anita almost loses interest. But not quite. She's staring fixedly at him, waiting for *any* movement.

'How about a coffee?' Vicky says brightly to keep Jerry talking. 'We make a great cappuccino right here in the kennel, don't we Steve?'

At a prod from Vicky, Steve, half-asleep, stirs in his chair. 'Er . . . what . . . oh, yeah, coffee. Thanks, Vicky. Nice idea. I *am* a bit thirsty. I'll have a cup. Terrific. Thanks.'

Only when Vicky secretly stamps on Steve's foot does he properly wake up.

'Uh! Oh, yeah. Coffee. You bet. You want it frothy, mate?'

Vicky, rolling her eyes, gives him a *get on with it* look.

Anita is kneeling beside Fred's cell now, still trying to get a response. This happens a lot. People can't quite believe he won't even stand up.

That's the moment Vicky gets called away by Jens to

help her deal with a troublesome cocker spaniel puppy. It leaves Sloppy Steve in charge of us.

Disaster.

'Nice coffee,' Jerry notes.

'Cheers,' Steve says, looking bored.

'Ahem,' Bessie chuffs at Anita. 'Someone else over here, in case you hadn't noticed! Since Fred couldn't care less, that is.'

Anita hears Bessie's bark and walks over. As soon as she's close enough, Bessie goes into her own performance.

Which, for Bessie, requires nothing more than just standing there looking . . . perfect.

Bessie won four separate prestige awards in her show-dog days, so she knows exactly how to look fantastic. She's what competition enthusiasts call a class-A dog, a best of breed.

Straightening her legs, she sets her tail like a raised sword. Then, standing in profile to the woman, she lifts her head *just so*.

And Anita is flabbergasted. Entranced. It's like a dog carved out of solid gold is standing in front of her. She actually staggers.

'My goodness, what a pretty . . . what a *beautiful* dog! What on earth is a miracle like her doing in here?'

And she's right to ask, because Bessie is a miracle. It's a complete disgrace that she's been stuck here at Happy Paws for two years. Except, of course, there

28

*is* a reason – and Anita's about to find out what it is.

'It's OK, Bessie,' Mitch says quickly, seeing her hackles beginning to rise. 'This woman looks OK to me. Stay cool.'

'I know,' Bessie growls, backing away as Anita gets closer. 'I'm fine. I'm fine. It's all right. I'm staying calm . . .'

Anita reads the warning written in great big letters above Bessie's cell:

### 'ATTENTION! BEWARE! DO NOT STROKE THIS DOG! NO HANDS THROUGH THE BARS!'

'Oh,' she pouts. 'Why can't Bessie be touched?'

The question is aimed at Sloppy Steve, but he doesn't hear it because a little boy has come crashing into the kennel. He's about five years old and the first thing he spots is a cake – a fresh cream and jam doughnut that Steve left on his chair.

Anita is still waiting for her answer, but that's not important to Steve. His eyes only see the cake. The possibility that the boy might eat his doughnut is unbearable to him.

'Leave it!' he squeals.

But the boy already has the cake in his hand. He's lifting it up, stuffing it into his mouth . . .

'NOOOOOOOOOOOO!' screams Steve. Grabbing what's left of the cake from the boy, he crams it straight into his own mouth.

29

'Er, excuse me,' Jerry says, not quite able to believe his eyes. 'Are you actually trying to eat that cake after the boy's been chewing it?'

Steve stops guiltily, crumbs and cream tumbling from his lips.

'It was *my* cake,' he whines. 'I didn't say the boy could have it, did I? I didn't *offer* it to him. I didn't hold it out and say, "You can have my cake", did I? I mean, it was *my* cake, yeah?' He stands there defiantly, bits of sugar and jam hanging off his chin. 'You're looking at me as if I nicked *his* cake. But I didn't, did I?'

Jerry just stares in amazement at Steve.

Mitch is enjoying the look on Steve's face. 'Go on, lick the jam off your chin, Stevie-boy,' he barks. 'You know you want to! Stuff it in! Waaaaaa! Waaaaaa! Go on!'

'Er, what about Bessie?' Anita says, still trying to get her answer. 'Can't I even get near her?'

'Yes, you certainly can get near her,' Bessie whispers, taking deep breaths now, steadying herself. 'Just give me one more second here, and I'll let you stroke me.'

It's obvious how much Anita likes the look of Bessie, and Bessie can see that as well, but it hardly makes any difference. She finds it almost impossible to let herself be petted. It's her original owner's fault. In preparation for the dog beauty pageants Bessie was entered into, she was obsessively brushed, blow-dried, tucked, cleaned and combed.

'My owner had a hundred different trimmers and metal combs,' Bessie told me once, with a shudder. 'But the worst thing was the *feathering*.'

'Feathering?'

'Hair extensions,' Bessie explained. 'She took hours over them. Twisting them into my hair – yanking, pulling, attaching steel clips.'

Bessie never got a break. Her owner would not stop primping and painfully pulling her hair until one day . . . Bessie lost it.

She *bit* her owner.

And now, even two years later, Bessie can still hardly bear to be touched. It makes her snappy. It makes her *angry*.

But I can see that she's trying extra hard today. Nobody understands better than Bessie that no one will take home a dog they can't even stroke and, despite her panic, Bessie knows only too well that a true, genuine dog-lover like Anita is her best chance in ages.

So, half-closing her eyes, she steels herself to be touched.

'There, there,' Anita says, pleased, and patting her. 'What's that silly notice doing over your cell? You're not so sensitive as all that . . .'

'It's OK,' Mitch says softly to Bessie. 'You can do it, you can.'

'I know,' Bessie groans, willing herself to stay still, but even as she says those words her legs are already starting to shake under Anita's fingers. And when Anita begins stroking her neck as well, Bessie suddenly shudders and gives me and Mitch a heartbreaking whine.

'I just . . . *can't*,' she whispers. 'Why won't she stop? Why do they always have to carry on petting me?'

The next instant her hackles fly up and Anita gasps as Bessie pulls back her lips and *snarls*.

'No, Bessie,' I hiss, but it's too late. Anita snatches her hand away as if she's been bitten by a snake.

The only chance now is if Steve can recover the situation; explain Bessie's problem.

That's when the little boy kicks him in the shin.

'Ooooaaarrrrh!' Steve groans, and the boy laughs gleefully.

Steve doesn't think. He just chases the boy out of the door and down the staircase. On the way the two of them crash into Vicky. There's a giant *OOOF* as they collide.

But it's all too late for Bessie. Jerry uses the distraction to get an arm around his wife's shoulder. 'This place is a madhouse, Anita,' he says. 'Total madhouse. We're out of here.'

By the time Vicky makes it back to us Anita is gone, and nobody is more upset about it than Bessie.

She heads to the corner of her cell and lies on her side, eyes staring into space.

I wait a few minutes, then whisper to her, 'Are you

all right, Bessie? You didn't want to be with them, anyway. That man wasn't a real dog-lover.'

Mitch says softly, 'Yeah, you were probably walking into a disaster with that one, Bess.'

'I know, boys, I know,' she whispers back, not looking at us. 'I'm just going to have a nap now, OK?'

'All right, Bess, you do that,' Mitch murmurs.

'Good idea,' I say, closing my eyes and wishing with all my heart that things were different for Bessie. How will she ever get a home if she can't get over her fear?

# Chapter Four

The kennel is quiet throughout lunchtime. At around two o'clock Mitch starts slapping himself with his paws, batting his head slowly from side to side. It's as he's going cross-eyed and – *bop, bop* – opening and closing his mouth like a fish that something amazing happens.

A family arrives to see me.

Actually, specifically, *me*.

This has not happened for so long that I don't know what to do. My scary face puts everyone off. No one ever comes to see me.

It's a youngish mum and her two daughters. The daughters both have straight, dark brown hair. The youngest looks to be about seven years old, her hair plaited and pinned with yellow butterfly ties. The older girl is around eleven, with a slim, freckled face and square, black-rimmed glasses. She looks very serious.

When they mention the 'Dog of the Month' page and ask for me, Vicky delays them. Even the photos on the website don't really prepare people for my facial injuries. Vicky knows they'll be shocked.

'Ralph's special,' I hear her explain from the office. 'Before you see him, let me tell you all the reasons why . . .'

Mitch and Bessie glance at each other. They know what a rare event this is.

'Hey, someone here for you, Ralph,' Bessie enthuses, rushing up to the bars between our cells to give me a comforting lick. 'They look . . . well, like a really nice family.'

'I know,' I say, trying not to get too excited.

They *do* look nice, too. Both girls are well-behaved, smiling politely at Vicky. At one point the older girl glances over her shoulder and gives me a bright smile, but I can see she's nervous.

Vicky takes her time. She's saying all sorts of nice

things about me, but she's also warning them what to expect when they get up close.

I don't feel ready for this. It's been so long.

'You'll be OK, mate,' Mitch says quietly, no longer bashing his head. 'You'll be fine. Just don't try the backflip.'

I nod, shaking a little. 'I'll just show them the right side of my face to start with. It's not so caved-in. Less scary.'

'It doesn't matter what part of you they see first, Ralph,' Bessie reassures me. 'Your pictures are on the website, remember? They glimpsed you coming in, too, and Vicky's preparing them. They're not going to run off.'

'OK,' I say. 'You're right. OK. OK . . .'

Feeling myself start to pant with anxiety, I hunker down on my haunches and take some deep breaths.

This is not the first time someone's come in especially to view me, but the last time was over a year ago. The man involved took one horror-filled glance and rushed straight out again. I'm always there to greet customers, of course. I'd never let Vicky down. I try. But I'm more used to people backing off in revulsion than smiling. And it's not as if I can put on a performance like Mitch, or a show-display like Bessie.

As Vicky opens the door to her office and leads the family out, I'm lying on my paws so they don't see me shaking.

Then, finding courage from somewhere, I creep up to my bars and give them a friendly *woof*.

It's an almost silent woof, of course, because I hurt my throat barking so much to get attention for my last owner, Muriel, when she was dying, but it's the best I can do. And I *can* make some noise. I'm not completely useless.

'It's fine, Ralph,' Mitch says. 'Just stay cool.'

Cool? My heart's pounding.

As the girls approach, I swallow, quickly twisting to show them the less collapsed side of my face.

'You look good, Ralph,' Bessie whispers. 'Just be yourself and they'll love you.'

The younger girl is scared of me. That's normal. Little kids are always scared of me.

'Look, Mummy.' She brings a hand up to her lips. 'He's got a broken face.'

'I know he has,' her mum says calmly. 'Vicky told us that, remember? He was in a fight. Another dog bit him. It wasn't his fault.'

'Is he a good dog, Mummy?'

'He's a very good dog. Shall we go and say hello to him? Vicky says he's friendly.'

The mum is standing behind the girls. I can see her trying to smile at me, but not quite managing it. I obviously look worse than she was expecting.

So far I haven't paid much attention to the older girl. She's wearing a metal bracelet with little dogs woven into it. She's not smiling but she doesn't look scared, either.

'There, have you both finished *staring* at him now?' she says to her mum and sister. 'I told you both to expect this. It's not Ralph's fault another dog attacked him. He was *saving a puppy's life*, remember? Let's stroke him.' But when she takes her little sister's wrist and tries to lead her towards me, it only panics her.

'Let me go!' she squeals. 'Mummy, I don't want to touch him! His face is all scrunched up! He's horrible! I hate him!'

'It's all right,' her mum says, giving Vicky an apologetic glance.

Vicky smiles, used to this. 'Oh, no problem at all,' she says lightly. 'It's fine. This often happens. It's the shock, that's all. She'll soon get used to that beaten-up face of Ralph's.'

Striding up to me, Vicky opens my cell door to show them how safe I am.

OK. My turn.

I stagger out. Bark in a friendly way.

'Oh, that's . . . an odd noise,' the mother says.

My soft, raspy bark always catches people by surprise.

The older daughter rolls her eyes. 'Mum! He *lost* his bark, remember? When he was stuck in that house trying to get help for his owner. His throat was *bleeding* when they found him, he'd been trying so hard. It's all on the website. I knew you hadn't read it properly. It's an amazing story. *He's* amazing.'

She walks straight up to me and gives me a confident pat on the head. Her fingers are gentle. She giggles briefly as she strokes my neck, excited.

'My name's Claire. Claire McCracken,' she says. 'It's an honour to meet such a brave dog.' She smiles, and I know what to do. I raise my right front paw and touch her knee. I've seen Mitch do the trick enough times.

'Look at that, Mum!' Claire cries, giving me a huge smile. 'See! He's smart, too. Isn't he great? We know how long Ralph's been in the kennel. What are we waiting for? Let's take him home right now.'

Vicky laughs.

So do Bessie and Mitch. None of us have ever heard a kid arguing so strongly for me before. Even Fred, pretending to be asleep in his cell, lets out a little chuckle.

Vicky almost hugs Claire.

'You're exactly right about him,' she says. 'So many people can't see past Ralph's face. Please come a little closer,' she encourages the younger sister. 'What's your name, by the way? You're very pretty.'

The girl shies away.

'Her name is Rowena,' Claire says. 'And she's tired today because she's been crying half the morning. Maybe she doesn't like her dress, or one of her dolls fell off the bed. It really could have been anything. She seems to have to cry every hour or she feels she's somehow *missed out*.'

Claire's mum gives Vicky a slightly pained smile and glances at Rowena.

Whatever she's like normally, Rowena is definitely crying now – big, splashy tears. The reason why isn't a mystery. It's me.

And now *I'm* scared. Because if Rowena gets too frightened, her mum will leave. I have to do something to make them like me . . . but what?

To reduce Rowena's terror, I get down as low as I can. That way I'm no higher than her knees. Then I shimmy across the floor, staying low, encouraging her to stroke me.

When I get too close she screams, slapping my head.

'Rowena!' her mum snaps.

'You horrible thing!' Claire shouts, grabbing her wrist.

'It's OK,' I woof. 'It didn't hurt!'

I can see how disturbed the mother is, and not just by Rowena's reaction. My head isn't the only ugly part of me. My body is short and long in all the wrong places as well. West Highland terrier. Schnauzer. Retriever. You name a breed, it seems to be mixed up in me.

Claire's mother frowns. It's obvious what she's thinking: why take a risk on an injured, ugly dog like me when there are plenty of healthier, more attractive dogs at Happy Paws to choose from? In fact, with eight full kennels, I wonder why she's bothering to look at me at all.

And then I understand why.

Of course.

It's not the mother who saw my details on the Happy Paws website.

It's Claire.

*She's* the one who knows all about me. She's obviously persuaded her family to come and visit me.

But now that her mum and Rowena have seen me in the flesh, things aren't working out so well.

Claire's mum reaches down to touch my ruined left cheek. She does it carefully, as if it must still hurt, but of course it doesn't any more so I let her. I nuzzle her hand – and she pulls away a bit.

Never mind. I wag my tail. It's a bit grim being the object of morbid fascination, but I'm used to it. If I can get her to keep stroking me for long enough, maybe she'll realise I'm a normal dog.

'What's wrong with Ralph's coat?' she asks Vicky.

Ah, here we go. My pale white body. My lack of hair.

'Mum, they *explained* all of that on the website,' Claire says in exasperation. 'If you'd bothered to read Ralph's medical history, you'd know that his coat was once a shiny, silky brown. It's a condition called growth hormone-responsive alopecia, and it's not *that* uncommon.' She strokes me again. 'His hair fell out over time, that's all. Which, if you ask me, just makes him look more interesting.'

I give Claire a little woof. I'm beginning to really like this girl.

'He's horrible!' Rowena screams as I shimmy closer to her.

'Be quiet, you!' Claire shouts.

How can I get Rowena to like me? I try turning over on my back and showing her my belly.

Rowena squirms away, but Claire gets down with me at once, laughing and rubbing my tummy with her fingers. Rowena backs off, hiding completely behind her mum now, begging to leave.

As I cower on the floor, trying not to whimper, trying not to beg, pushing my paws into Claire's body to stay close to the only one who really likes me, Bessie shakes her head at Rowena. 'Ralph, Ralph, Ralph,' she murmurs, while all Mitch can do is stare sadly at me.

It all ends with Claire's mum giving me a brittle smile. 'Well, thank you,' she says to Vicky. 'It's been a pleasure meeting Ralph. He looks like a lovely dog. He really does. But I don't think, right now, he's quite the dog for us.'

'Mum, no!' Claire shouts. 'He is. He IS!'

'No, I think . . .' her mum says, 'I really think we should go.'

And she does, with Rowena gleefully running ahead of her.

Claire, though, refuses to leave. She has to be bodily hauled out by her mum.

After the kennel door closes and the sound of Claire's screaming has receded, I slowly rise to my feet and glance up.

Giving me the tenderest of glances, Vicky puts her arms around me. Everyone else looks devastated. Bessie and Mitch's tails are sunk between their legs. Even Sloppy Steve looks pale.

'Well,' I say, walking as steadily as I can back into my cell and collapsing on the floor. 'That's that, then.'

# Chapter Five

Not many other people come into our kennel that afternoon, and I'm glad. At around half past two, a weird lady wanders in wanting to know if we can sell her some live mice for her pet anaconda snake.

'No,' Vicky tells her. 'We only have live snakes that eat people!'

Later in the afternoon, a couple strolls in searching for – guess what? – puppies.

'Ickle puppies!' I manage to sing weakly, but I do it from under my blanket, and I stay in that blankety darkness most of the afternoon, feeling miserable. It's not as if I haven't been rejected countless times before, but this time it really hurts because . . . well, no one has ever wanted me like Claire McCracken before.

I ignore Bessie's whispers of affection and Mitch's attempts to get me to laugh, and finally I'm led out for a walk.

Whenever she's on shift, no matter how busy she is, Vicky always takes each of us across the main road to Grace Park. Fred sometimes refuses to go these days, but usually Vicky can persuade even him to go on a gentle, stiff-legged stroll. We only get about half an hour in the park, but it's still good to be outside, especially today. I'm always leashed, of course. Vicky would love to let me run free, but she'd be sacked if she ever let me off the lead. It's against the rules. Too many dogs run away.

Today, I feel like running away too.

When we get back – both of us cold because it's chilly out there – Cleo, one of the new puppies we were expecting, is being led in by Jens. Any new dog is a welcome break from the kennel's monotony but, after my rejection earlier, I'm especially pleased to see a fresh face.

Cleo is a shy, shuffling basset hound. Like all bassets she's close to the ground, with a big, droopy-cheeked, sad-looking face. She can't be more than six or seven months old and, as Jens walks her in, she's nervous, head bowed, glancing anxiously at each of us.

'Hi,' I say, trying to put her at ease.

'Er . . . hello,' she answers in the smallest of voices.

45

She stops to stare at me. My wrecked face shocks dogs just as much as people.

Bessie, wagging her tail, says to her, 'Had a difficult time? Don't worry, you're safe with us.'

'That's right!' Mitch says. 'Nice to meet you. You're welcome here.'

We always greet new dogs affectionately. It's such a scary thing, entering Happy Paws for the first time. Dogs find themselves unexpectedly dumped here, stuck with strangers, with no idea what's going to happen to them. No wonder they're scared.

But Cleo is *really* scared. Puppies often are. One reason so many of them stay with us when kennel three is full is that Vicky is better than the other managers at making youngsters feel at home.

'Cleo was found tied to a tree in Gurney Wood ten days ago,' Vicky tells Steve, reading the notes passed from Assessment – where all new dogs at Happy Paws go first to be checked. 'She was shivering when they found her. Thirsty, as well. She had a name badge, but no contact or owner information. Poor thing.'

Softly lowering her hand towards Cleo, Vicky lets her sniff.

'What's your story, then?' she says, stroking Cleo's flank. 'You're not even quite sure about me being this close, are you? Let's go in the chill room, get to know each other.'

The chill room is a small area attached to kennel

five, full of soft furnishings and toys. Vicky created it especially for dogs like Cleo, youngsters who need a bit of privacy and reassurance, and she keeps it heated at all times. We can't go in there often – Happy Paws regulations mean we're stuck in our cells during visiting hours – but at quiet times Vicky ignores that rule and often lets us get together to play and chill out.

I can see how nervous Cleo is by the way she only very timidly lets Vicky lead her inside. She's walking quietly on her sharp nails, trying to make no noise at all.

Afterwards, Vicky puts down a fresh blanket and leads Cleo into the cell next to Bessie's. Cleo nuzzles the treat Vicky leaves her and buries her nose inside her blanket, glancing around warily.

Two minutes later the second dog arrives.

It's a boy this time. Young again, less than a year old, but much more confident than Cleo. In he comes, a youthful bounce in his step.

'Ravi,' Vicky reads from his description.

I can't help smiling. His name suits him. He's a red and white springer spaniel, and right away I can see he's typical for his breed – full of energy.

'Hiya,' Mitch barks, recognising a kindred spirit. 'I like your Christian Dior collar. Where did you get that from, then?'

'My owner.'

'Ah. What happened to him?'

'Don't know. Disappeared. My fault,' Ravi says dolefully. 'At least I think it was my fault. I was chasing a cat at the time.'

'Chasing a cat?' Mitch laughs, throwing his head back. 'You can never be blamed for that, son. They *ask* for it.'

Ravi gazes up in wonder. 'Do they? I thought it was just me being mad.'

'Then we're *both* mad,' Mitch chuckles. 'Anyway, friendly rivalry is all part of the great dog–cat tradition. They'd be bored to death without us.'

Ravi gives Mitch a big, wide grin.

'No major issues for this one,' Vicky reads from Assessment's notes. 'Oh, wait. There's one thing – cats. They're not sure how he is with them. He needs a proper test. OK, I'll arrange it.'

'Why've these puppies come to us at all?' Sloppy Steve moans. 'We only got rid of the last lot of dogs a few days ago.'

'Because kennel three is full right now,' Vicky tells him, an edge to her voice. 'And because we love any and all dogs, don't we, Steve? We can't wait to help them. Which is why we work here.'

That shuts Steve up.

Mitch flicks his tongue out. 'So, you're a fellow cat-chaser,' he chuffs, giving Ravi a nod of respect. 'Good to hear. Are there any breeds you especially like to go after?'

'I'm not fussy,' Ravi tells him.

'Me, neither. Though given a free choice I'd pick a Siamese.'

'I've never met one of those,' Ravi says keenly. 'What are they like?'

'Oh, you'll like chasing those,' Mitch says. 'Thin, noisy, hissy things, they are. Squashed-up, whiskery faces. Mincy types. Practically begging to be chased! Voices like snakes. "I'm so delightfully pretty." You know the way cats always talk. "My tail's so beautiful and long. My eyes are so shiny." In love with themselves . . .'

'Yeah!' Ravi agrees. 'Cats are weird. Slinking about in that slow way they have, as if they own the place.'

'You've got their characters nailed, Ravi,' Mitch tells him. 'I can see right away you're one of the smarter dogs we've had in here. I knew a Burmese Blue once. Basked every night outside my window, she did, teasing me.'

'Sounds annoying.'

'Exactly. And you know the most annoying thing about that Burmese Blue cat, Ravi? It wasn't even blue! It was grey. So *pretentious*!'

Cleo isn't saying anything to all of this, but I can see her listening closely. She's curious – and enjoying the friendly chat. I'm not even sure she knows that over the last few minutes she's been edging across her cell towards Bessie an inch at a time, until now they're almost touching. Bessie pretends she hasn't noticed, then very softly lays her paw on Cleo's through the bars.

Fred, meantime, is scowling from his corner cell. He's always disliked puppies. I've no idea why.

'So how come you're stuck in here?' Ravi asks Mitch. 'A great dog like you . . . it's hard to believe.'

When he hears that, laughter fires like a gunshot from Fred's cell. It makes Ravi and Cleo jump.

'I'll tell you why Mitch is still stuck here,' Fred scoffs. 'Because he's a loony cat-chaser, like you, that's why. Listen to you both. "Practically begging to be chased!" Eight families have taken Mitch so far, but like an idiot he just runs off after any old mangy cat. Pretty soon he ends up back here again. It's pathetic.'

Fred's drooling as he says this. He always drools when he gets excited.

Ravi is taken aback by the nasty tone of Fred's outburst. He looks offended on Mitch's behalf.

Mitch, though, is used to it. He laughs ruefully. 'Got to admit the old fella over there has a point,' he says, smiling crookedly. 'I see those fluffy faces and it's like they're taunting me. To be honest, I don't know why all their owners make such a fuss over me chasing them. It's not as if I hurt the cats. The last thing I want is a wad of their fur in my mouth. It's just a little chase. Most cats love the excitement. Well, some of them . . .'

'You make it all sound like a *laugh*,' Fred says bitterly. 'Like one of your stupid jokes. But it's not.'

He drools some more, then growls at both puppies, 'You're in a home for unwanted dogs now. Note the word *unwanted*. As in *nobody wants you*. Get it? You were dumped here. That means no one cares about you. Everyone is looking for the perfect dog and, trust me, with all the choices here, you're not likely to be it.'

Fred is in full stride now, froth leaping from his lips. Listening to him, Cleo shrinks back into her cell so far that you can hardly see her. Ravi just looks shaken.

'What Mitch won't tell you,' Fred barks on, 'is that he's dangerously close to being considered *unrehomable*. And when that happens our vet, T-bone, is asked to get out his shiny little needle and use it to put the dog down. Put it to sleep. Kill it.'

Silence follows. Both puppies are shocked. And Fred, gnarly old codger that he is, is rather pleased about that.

'And what's more—'

'Rragh! Stop! *Right now!*'

It's Bessie, growling from deep in her throat. 'Enough! Not one more word, Fred!' She's almost shaking with anger. 'I mean it!'

She snarls at him then, and Bessie does that so rarely to another dog that Fred cowers. Once he's retreated to the back of his cell, Bessie turns back to both puppies.

'Now, listen to me carefully,' she tells them. 'That's all nonsense. The only dogs I've ever seen put down at

Happy Paws were ones so abused and mistreated that they couldn't even be handled by kennel staff. That doesn't apply to either of you lovely puppies, so just forget everything Fred said. He's not . . . he's not quite himself lately, that's all.'

That afternoon – while Vicky takes both puppies down to T-bone to receive an anti-parvo virus shot – Bessie confronts Fred directly.

'Shame on you,' she murmurs. 'Scaring young dogs like that on their first day here. Especially Cleo. You can see how sensitive and vulnerable she is. As if she's not scared enough.'

Fred won't look at her, but Bessie isn't finished with him yet.

'Is misery really the only thing that gets you animated these days?' she challenges him. 'We both know it's young dogs you dislike, and we both know why, don't we? I've let it go until now, Fred, but I'm tired of you terrifying every youngster who comes into the kennel. Now, we'll say no more about this, but no more frightening these two puppies while they're here.'

Fred makes no reply. He just sits in his cell with his head turned to the wall.

I'm intrigued, to be honest. Fred's never explained to me or Mitch how he ended up at Happy Paws, but I think it had something to do with a younger dog. He only told Bessie the full story a couple of years ago when he was particularly miserable. I heard the sob in his voice that night, the only time I've ever heard Fred cry.

Bessie's kept his secret, though – and, knowing her, she always will.

Vicky is the last to leave every evening, and by ten to six today she's ready to go.

The puppies look worried as she gathers up her jacket and starts to close everything down, but Vicky's left them treats and we've been reassuring them as well, so that when she blows us all a last kiss and switches off the lights Cleo and Ravi don't whimper too much.

*Snap.*

Darkness, except for our little window. In the summer we get lots of daylight, but at this time of year 'lights off' means exactly that.

The sudden darkness always comes as a shock to new arrivals. Sitting upright in their cells, Cleo and Ravi look spooked. They keep blinking at the window, trying to wring as much comfort as they can from the orange streetlight glow.

After we calm them down, Ravi finally gets up the confidence to say, 'Ralph, I hope you don't mind me asking, but . . . what happened to your fur?'

I wink at Mitch and he winks back. These puppies

don't need any more sad stories right now. Time to give them something to smile about instead.

'It's a terribly tragic story,' I sigh. 'One day I was a full-coated, magnificent specimen, my hair beautiful and glossy. Then, over several years, the hair just . . .' I throw my paws over my eyes dramatically '. . . fell out.'

'I remember the final little tuft well,' Mitch says, staring sad-eyed into the distance. 'A frizzy brown clump, it was. The patch was on Ralph's bum, I seem to remember.'

'My left cheek,' I say.

'Yes, indeed,' Mitch continues wistfully. 'His left cheek. Ralph would sometimes catch sight of it in a mirror as he was passing, and whenever he did he'd stop and swing his rear end around, trying to get a better look at it, so proud, so proud. And then . . .'

'And then,' I sniff, 'the last fluffy tuft fell out.'

This time Ravi laughs.

'Yes, heart-rending it was,' Mitch says. 'There'd been a story in Ralph's family. Of an ancient ancestor – the so-called "bald dog". Hushed up, it was, a source of shame, but they always feared that Great Uncle Hairless would return to haunt the family.'

The puppies are both smiling now. They know a good story when they hear one. Shy Cleo starts walking around her cell, her own problems at least momentarily forgotten. Ravi grins in the dark, eager for more.

'And what . . . what happened to your face, Ralph?' he asks. 'How did that happen?'

Ah. My pretty face. I don't like to talk about that much. No funny memories there.

Bessie steps in. 'Ralph was less than a year old when a big mastiff attacked a little puppy close to him,' she tells them quietly. 'Against such a dog, Ralph must have been tempted to run away. Instead,' she glances proudly at me, 'he dived in to protect the puppy. That saved the puppy's life, but the mastiff went for Ralph instead, and before it could be pulled off . . . well, it hurt him badly.'

Both new dogs give me a respectful nod, but I can see the story has brought back Cleo's fear. She stares at me, her tail firmly between her legs. 'When we were in Assessment we heard some scary things,' she says, 'about there being more dogs needing homes than there are people who want them. Is that true?'

They glance at Fred, but ever since Bessie had a go at him he's stayed silent.

'You'll both be fine,' Bessie reassures them. 'Puppies your age usually get homes within six weeks, and Vicky can normally do better than that. Just *no biting*, OK?'

'No biting?' Ravi says, confused.

'I mean you must never, ever bite a visitor while you're here,' Bessie explains. 'Happy Paws have a "Do Not Destroy" policy. That means that unless a dog is too aggressive to handle they'll never be put down. But if you bite a person – even if it's in self-defence or a mistake – the staff can't be sure they can safely rehome you, and they *will* put you down. It's the rule here.' She smiles to soften her words. 'But don't worry. As long as you avoid doing something silly like that, you'll both get a home, I promise.'

Her promise hangs tantalisingly in the air. And because it's Bessie who gives it you can see the puppies relaxing.

A little later, I ask them about what they liked to do on the outside. About their hopes for the future as well. About their dreams. It's important to keep young dogs thinking about those things. They can get despondent quickly in here.

It turns out – no surprise – that Cleo just wants to be in a safe place with someone who really likes her.

Ravi, of course, can't see beyond chasing things.

'But never mind us, what about you?' Cleo asks. She nudges Bessie. 'What are *your* dreams?'

Tucking her long bushy tail underneath her, Bessie sighs. 'I'm like you, Cleo. I don't need much, just a home. On cold winter nights like these I wouldn't say no to an open fire, though – and maybe a tad more variety in the food department.' She grins. 'Binky's chunks can get a bit wearing.'

Ravi raises his head. 'How about you, Mitch?'

'Well, I do have this brilliant dream where I'm in a house full of cats,' Mitch confesses. 'I'm the only

56

dog and there are at least ten cats, sometimes twenty or more. I chase them into the bedrooms, the kitchen, the cellar, everywhere. They never get tired of it and neither do I.' He lets his tongue dangle. 'It's just an everlasting chase.'

Ravi laughs, then yawns loudly and snaps his jaws shut. 'You haven't said anything yet, Ralph.'

'Me?' I scratch my chin, nudging the blankets on my bed. 'Oh, I just want to run around.'

'To run around?'

'Yeah. I've never been able to do that.'

Ravi's puzzled. 'How come?'

'My original owner, Muriel, always kept me on a lead,' I tell him. 'She was afraid I'd get lost, so she used the lead on every walk.'

'You've *never* been off-lead? You're joking!'

'No.' I smile at the shocked look on Ravi's face. 'I came straight to Happy Paws after Muriel died. The dogs aren't allowed off-lead here. They can't afford for us to run off and bite someone or cause an accident. So that's my dream. I'd like to have the freedom to just run around.'

'Where would you run to, Ralph?' Cleo asks, blinking at me.

I think about that and, when I answer, even Fred laughs.

*'Everywhere.'*

57

# Chapter Six

'You know what, Ralph?' Mitch says, scratching his left ear faster than a hummingbird. 'Last night I dreamt a massive crocodile, wrapped in a burger bun, was chasing me down the street saying, "Eat me, eat me." I can't decide if it was a good dream or not. What do you think?'

It's quarter past eight the next morning and Mitch is already banging into the walls, buzzing and talking non-stop.

But I'm not really listening because I'm missing Cleo. She was transferred to the puppy enclosure first thing today. It often happens like that – the puppies always get moved in there if a spot opens up. They're much happier being all together, so it's great for Cleo, but she was a lovely pup and I miss her.

There's another reason I'm mostly ignoring Mitch, though.

I'm practising my backflip.

I've decided it's the key to me finding a way out of here. Bessie has her looks. Mitch has The Performance. But me, with my beaten-up face, well, I need to distract people, to *dazzle* them. I've tried just being friendly, but where's that got me? Even when someone like Claire McCracken comes along, it still isn't enough.

The trouble is, I can't do the backflip yet. My legs are too weak from being stuck in here all these years.

'You OK?' Ravi asks me, seeing me practising half-jumps.

'Fine,' I say.

Mitch frowns. 'Fine for a grasshopper, maybe. You're not built like Wally the whippet, mate. You're only hurting yourself.'

Ignoring him, I close my eyes and leap backwards again.

'Yowwwwl!' I scream as I land on my nose.

Mitch winces.

'Did I *nearly* do it that time?' I ask.

'No, mate,' he says. 'You just jumped up in the air and landed on your face again.'

Bessie knows this is important to me. 'Maybe try rocking backwards and forwards on your haunches to get up momentum before you do the jump part,' she says, hardly able to watch.

'Good idea.'

I try that. Land on my muzzle.

'Rrrruuuuuu!'

After a few more tries my nose is so bruised that it's swelling up. I don't care, though. That humiliating visit from Claire's family has only made me realise that I have to master the backflip even if it kills me.

By the time Vicky comes on shift I'm trembling with exhaustion.

Hurrying past Steve – who hasn't even noticed what I'm doing – Vicky enters my cell. She examines my head bruises and kneels beside me.

'You look like you've been beating yourself up, Ralph,' she whispers. 'What's going on?'

'Mrrrrmm,' I sigh, and leave my head in her arms, letting her stroke me.

But all I can think about is the backflip.

The rest of the morning is quiet, so I have a rest. At about half past eleven Vicky goes on a break, and while she's out we get a call on the internal phone. Annoyed at having to pick the phone up at all, Sloppy Steve reluctantly listens to the message. Finally putting the phone down, he sighs and scrawls on the board:

# RAVI — CAT TEST. 12.15 TODAY.

'Great, great!' Ravi says, liking the sight of his name up on the board. 'Cat test. Sounds brilliant. Do I get to chase one?'

He hasn't noticed that we've all stopped chomping on our tasteless Binky's 'mouth-watering smackarooni bites'.

'He doesn't understand,' Bessie mutters to me. 'He thinks the cat test is a game.' She quickly turns to Mitch. 'Twelve fifteen. That only gives us just over half an hour to get him ready. Can we do it?'

'Depends on who the cat is,' Mitch says thoughtfully. 'Who are they using these days?'

I scratch my head. 'The last few cat tests have been with . . . oh, what's his name? Tiddles? Toddles? Toodlies? Something like that. He's ancient. Normally sleeps through the test. We can prepare Ravi for that, surely?'

'Hold on,' Bessie says in a low tone. 'Oh, please, no. Please, please, no . . .'

Sloppy Steve has written something else on the board. The cat assigned to the test:

## OLIVIA DARLING SPARKLE.

'OMG,' Mitch murmurs.
Fred, from his corner, starts laughing darkly.

'Anything but *that* cat,' Bessie groans, closing her eyes. 'Even I can't handle Olivia.'

Ravi is amused by the shock on our faces. 'Olivia Darling Sparkle,' he says. 'That's a nice name. What's the matter with you guys? What is she? A tiger, or something?'

'Worse than that,' I tell him. 'Even dogs who *like* cats end up attacking Olivia. She loves causing dogs to fail the cat test. It's what she lives for. Only one dog this year passed the cat test with her. That was Oscar, a husky.'

'Who was deaf,' Mitch reminds me.

'You guys are kidding, right?' Ravi says, clearly enjoying the drama. 'Why all the fuss? What is this cat test, anyway?'

'The cat just sits in a box in the middle of a room,' I tell him. 'Then you're taken in there on a lead, and the staff watch to see how you react.'

'And then I go after the cat, yeah?' Ravi says. 'Rip the box open, chase it around . . .'

'No.' I shake my head. 'This is important, Ravi. If you want to get out of Happy Paws quickly, don't go for the cat.'

'But Ralph, if I see one—'

Mitch jumps forward, kicking his bowl to get Ravi's attention. 'No, listen,' he tells him firmly. 'Lots of people who want a dog from Happy Paws already have a cat at home.'

'Really?' Ravi looks amazed.

'I know,' Mitch says. 'Sounds weird, huh? But they're animal-lovers, remember. That's why they come to Happy Paws in the first place. And many of them are looking for a nice dog to be super-friendly with their cat.'

Ravi's tail shoots straight down. 'You're joking!'

'I'm not. They want a dog to keep their kitty company.'

Ravi laughs. 'Brilliant joke, Mitch. That's just about the funniest thing I've ever heard.'

'I'm not joking,' Mitch tells him. 'Some owners hope you and the cat will become best friends.'

'Best . . . best friends?'

'Yeah. They want you and the cat to lie all close and happy together by the fire. In fact, some of them *buy* a fire just to see you do that. They buy special soft cushions as well.'

'Why?'

'So you can sleep side by side. So you can *snuggle*.'

'That's crazy!' Ravi lets out a half-amused, half-outraged grunt. 'I can't go to a home with crazy owners, Mitch.'

'It's your best shot for getting out of here,' I mutter. 'Mitch is right, Ravi. You *can* learn not to chase cats.'

'No, no, I can't do it!' Ravi says. 'The hair, the smell . . .'

'You can!' Mitch says sternly. 'Overall, it's fun to chase them, but if you leave a cat alone it'll generally

63

leave you alone, too. And a cat-friendly dog is much easier to place in a new home, OK? So today, in the test, you've just got to prove one thing – that you can avoid getting too excited when you see the cat. That's all.'

Ravi is a bit put out by all of this. 'Er . . . OK, Mitch,' he says. 'I'm sure I can do that. If you say so. Right. Fine. I'll just do . . . nothing. How hard can that be?'

'You've got no idea,' Bessie says. 'This is no ordinary cat.'

Fifteen minutes later, Jens arrives. She's carrying Olivia Darling Sparkle in a big wooden box. The box has wire mesh sides so you can see the cat inside.

Olivia Darling Sparkle is sitting on her generous-sized bum, looking spectacularly relaxed and comfy. She's a Persian longhair. A pedigree. Expensive to buy. In my experience a lot of pedigree cats are stuck up, prissy and mean. Olivia Darling Sparkle makes those other pedigree cats look friendly.

She's big and grey, with a wide face. A wide, fat, squashed-up face with a permanent smile plastered across it.

She's easily the most confident cat I've ever met. Some cats swell up like a hairy balloon when they first see us, hissing and spitting with fear. There's none of that with Olivia Darling Sparkle. Nothing seems to frighten her. You'd think that being brought into a kennel full of dogs and being outnumbered five to one would at least make her a bit anxious, but I can already hear her purring.

It's a purr of excitement.

She loves these moments. Her huge, slow-blinking, almond-shaped green eyes are already fully dilated, scanning us, trying to pinpoint her victim. And I can smell her as well – the normal cat smell, but sweeter. Mitch's nostrils quiver with distaste.

Jens puts Ravi on a lead, keeping a tight hold, and places the box with Olivia Darling Sparkle inside his cell.

Ravi, strolling up, gives Olivia Darling Sparkle a couple of casual sniffs, then pretends to be more interested in his dog bowl.

Which is perfect. It's what we've told him to do. You can show an interest – every dog is bound to if a cat's left near them – but the staff want to see that you are only intrigued. That's what they're looking for. Mild to medium-level curiosity. Nothing more.

'Remember what I told you,' Mitch says. 'Stay cool.'

'Yeah, yeah,' Ravi replies.

Olivia Darling Sparkle hasn't said a word so far. She's following Ravi with eyes narrowed like a lizard's, sizing him up. When she realises he's not going to dive straight at the box she looks pleased.

'Ahhhhh,' she says, glancing at Mitch. 'Been coaching him, have you? Despite which, I can tell he's dying to jump at me. How are you doing, anyway, Mitch? Still ramming your teeth up against the bars of your cage?'

Mitch grins.

'This puppy needs to pass the test,' I say. 'Be good, Olivia.'

'Be good?' She smiles expansively. 'You're still here as well, Ralph, are you? Honestly, dear, if I had a face like yours I'd shave my rear end and learn to walk backwards. And I see Fred's still with us as well, though whether he's dead or alive these days is anyone's guess.'

Fred laughs. We've been trading sharp insults like this with Olivia for many years. She's a No-Hoper like us. Way too fussy to stay in a new home for long. And secretly – though she'd never admit it – I suspect she has a soft spot for us.

'Ah, Bessie's here, too,' Olivia says. 'Pretty girl like you still stuck with the No-Hopers, eh? Where's your class, girl? You could have had any home you wanted. A nice big place in the country. Your own grounds to walk around. Steak to eat every day. Instead, you're still in here, your breath smelling of Binky's stale chicken. So sad.'

'What about you, then?' Bessie says, unfazed. 'A prized Persian pedigree and you're still at Happy Paws.

Can't find a home when ragged, common tabbies are going every day.'

'Oh, I don't want to ever *go home*,' Olivia Darling Sparkle purrs mildly back. 'Why would I want to do that when I can stay here and make sure as many dogs as possible *never get to go home*?'

Olivia doesn't really mean that. She's just baiting us. But she's serious about the cat test. As the oldest cat in Happy Paws she sees it as her sacred duty to protect other cats, especially kittens, from unsafe dogs. I can see why she's suspicious of Ravi. Despite Mitch's coaching, he can't wait to get closer to her. He likes chasing cats a bit too much for his own good.

When he next wanders up to her box, Olivia surprises him by suddenly poking her tail out and *twitching* it in his face.

Ravi is annoyed, but a sharp look from Mitch keeps him from reacting.

Olivia smiles, all her teeth showing, then lifts a single heavy paw through the box and cuffs him a few times.

She does it gently, but Ravi immediately jumps at her and growls.

'Oooh, this one's definitely not yet ready for the beautiful and perfect world of cats,' Olivia pouts. 'He's way too feisty. What if I gave you a kitten to lie beside?' she purrs at him. 'All snuffly, with sleepy-soft whiskers. How does that sound to you, little boy?'

'Not good,' Ravi says.

'I thought not.'

Olivia Darling Sparkle sighs, sounding disappointed. Turning to me, she lets her tongue dance across the surface of her very white, very clean teeth.

'I'm not even having to spit or hiss to get him to react,' she says. 'I'm sorry, but this one is way too yappy and full of himself. He needs to learn a little more respect before he's ready to be with us felines.'

'No, no,' I say quickly. 'Ravi's . . . fine, Olivia. Or he will be. Bessie and I are already talking to him about it. He's just a chaser. We'll straighten him out, I promise.'

But Olivia Darling Sparkle is not convinced, and when Olivia is not convinced she turns into something that's more like a claws-out panther than a cat.

I watch as her face hardens, her tail falling perfectly still.

'Such silly long legs you have, puppy-boy,' she says to Ravi in a sudden hissy-whisper. 'Was your father a chicken?'

'Don't listen to a word she says!' Mitch growls.

'It's OK, I can handle this,' Ravi declares, looking more confident with every second. He steps towards Olivia, gazes disdainfully at her. 'Is that the best you can do? "Was your father a chicken?" Well, I've got news for you. My father was a great guy.'

Olivia Darling Sparkle pokes out her pale pink tongue. 'Oh, I'm so glad to hear that. Braver than his chicken son, then, who's so afraid of me he won't even come close in case he gets a weeny scratch on his nose.'

Ravi's face drains of colour. 'What?' he barks, outraged. 'I'm not afraid!'

'Easy now,' Jens says, grabbing his lead as he strains to reach the box. 'What's suddenly got into you? You were doing so well.'

Ravi manages to restrain himself.

Laughing, Olivia slowly turns her back on him, twitching her tail in his face.

'Oh, he's really not worth my attention at all,' she murmurs. 'Actually, Mitch, darling, can I just ask you to back away from me a little? I know you're eager to help your little puppy-boy, but you do smell rather like a dead mouse that's been stuck inside one of Sloppy Steve's socks for a year.'

At that insult to Mitch, Ravi can't hold back any more. He heaves on his lead, barking non-stop, nearly pulling Jens over.

Olivia Darling Sparkle shakes her head. 'What are you trying to do, you silly baby? The box is shut. You can't get at me.'

But Ravi isn't listening any more. He's just pulling like crazy, trying to get at Olivia.

Even with two hands on his lead Jens can barely hold him back. 'Steve, you'd better get Olivia out of here,' she says sadly. 'Ravi's definitely not suitable for cats. Pity.'

Job done, and safe in her box, Olivia Darling Sparkle yawns. Then, preening herself with a single paw, she waves an almost fond farewell to us all.

As she's being carried out like a royal princess, she takes the trouble to nod to Ravi. Purring, she twitches her whiskers at him. 'No offence,' she says, 'but the neighbourhood cats will only torment you if you can't resist a few insults. I'm sure you'll do better next time. Goodbye, now.'

With that Olivia blows Ravi a kiss, and the last we see of her is that long, superior grey tail of hers, tapping the inside of the box as she swishes it smoothly from side to side.

# Chapter Seven

Next morning Ravi is still a bit down about his failure in the cat test, but he's not feeling too bad because Mitch has convinced him that a young feisty dog like him really had no chance against an old pro like Olivia Darling Sparkle.

'And anyway,' Mitch admits, 'if you hadn't gone for her, I'd have been very disappointed.'

Shortly after that a poodle goes home from kennel three, which means that Jens can squeeze Ravi into the puppy enclosure. The great news we hear is that Ravi will get a place near Cleo, but even if he didn't have

Cleo for company we're not worried for him. Ravi's such a friendly, well-adjusted youngster that he should be snapped up in no time by a good family.

It's still sad when Jens comes to take him away, though. Especially for Mitch. He's formed a really close attachment to Ravi. Not that he shows that as Ravi's led out. 'Don't forget to make friends with as many cats as you can,' he says, with a wink.

'I will, Mitch,' Ravi replies, and they both laugh.

'And don't forget . . .' Bessie reminds him.

'I know!' Ravi rolls his eyes. '*Never bite a person!*'

'Unless it's someone like Sloppy Steve,' Mitch adds, 'as he'll be too lazy to do anything about it.'

'Not even then,' Bessie calls out cheerily, and there's more of the same until finally, in a flurry of our good wishes and barks of affection, Ravi is out of the door and gone.

Even Fred seems thoughtful once he's left. Unusually, he raises his head long enough to say, 'That boy will find a home for sure, and deserve to.'

Which sort of expresses how we all feel.

After Ravi goes, I spend a while strenuously practising my backflip. Bessie's supervising me closely today, increasingly worried I'm going to injure myself, but even with her help I still keep landing flat on my face.

The noise of my chin smacking against the floor finally wakes Sloppy Steve.

Because Vicky's out at the time, he yells from his chair, 'Oy, shut it! I'm tired, all right! I'm really, really tired! I still haven't even finished this biscuit. All I'm asking for is a few seconds of peace to finish this one shortbread biscuit, and maybe this cake as well. That's two *tiny* things, all right?'

He's still moaning when Vicky arrives with a new dog in tow.

Paolo.

A dachshund.

Dark brown. Short. Tiny legs. Big eyelashes. Built like a sausage. That about sums him up.

He's not much to look at in terms of size but, boy, that is not what Paolo himself thinks. He's swaggering and preening the second he's in the door.

'He's from the southern part of the United States originally,' Vicky reads from Assessment's notes. 'Spent several years in Italy, too. An American-Italian mix. No one seems to know why his owners gave him up. Apparently, when they dropped him off, they just put their hands over their ears and ran out.' She frowns. 'Ran out? That's weird. But looking at his record, Paolo's had quite a few owners. Mm, I wonder why he keeps getting dumped.'

It's certainly not obvious to us dogs either when we first meet Paolo.

'He's good-looking, isn't he?' Bessie whispers. She's just talking to herself, but she accidentally says it loud enough for Mitch and me to hear.

'Ooooh, got a boyfriend now, have you?' Mitch says, grinning away.

'Don't be silly,' Bessie says, rolling her eyes, but she definitely likes the look of Paolo, that's for sure.

And Paolo very much seems to notice Bessie as well. Oh, yes.

'Ciao, baby. Ciao, ciao, nice to meet ya,' he says, his voice deep and rich for a little guy. He has a strong accent, too. A deep d-r-a-w-l. Definitely from the south of the USA. I met a dog from Alabama once who sounded a bit like him, but it's weird because Paolo sprinkles Italian words in there as well.

'Oh, yeah, just got in from New York via Venice, Italy,' he tells us. 'Lots of shiny tourist attractions. Lots of pigeons to chase. Oh, yeah. Sunshine and blue skies. Groovy.'

*Groovy?* Is this guy for real? Mitch and I chuckle.

Once he's led to his cell, Paolo gives us a confident grin and licks a tongueful of water from his bowl. 'Ah, nice and cool. *Refresheratto.*' His muzzle comes up dripping. 'Like the Trevi fountain in Rome, or the Great Lakes of Canada, the deepness of which I have seen for myself. Have you witnessed those tremendous bodies of water, Bessie?'

'No, I haven't, Paolo,' Bessie says, batting her

74

eyelashes at him. 'But I'd like to. Do tell me more.'

'A pleasure, young lady.' Paolo bows and flicks some drips of water over me without noticing. 'But first, does my hair look shiny to you, Bessie? I ask because I received a wholesome bath upon arrival here, but the shampoo they used dried my coat out something fearful. My fur, especially along my tummy, came out all scrunchy and ruffled, and they didn't even clip my nails afterwards. I like my nails done a special way. I'm sure you do, too, baby – not too close to the paw – am I right?'

'Er, actually, I've not had my nails clipped in a while,' Bessie says.

'Me neither,' Mitch pipes up, 'but I like them to be polished afterwards, don't you, Ralph?'

'Definitely,' I say. 'And painted green, so they match my eyes.'

'That's very interesting,' Paolo says to me, not getting the humour at all. 'A dog's got to keep up his appearance, hasn't he? Where would we be without our looks? Mere street-trash. I may be an eight-year-old dog but I still have my good features and, while I do say so myself, many of the ladies over the years have taken a shine to me on that account.'

Even Bessie laughs this time.

'Yes, Paolo, I can see why,' she says. 'What you lack in height you make up for in . . . in confidence.'

'Thank you, baby.' Paolo shows his perfect white teeth as he grins at Bessie. 'I like you, too. Now let me tell you about the time I sailed from Naples, with the wind whistling through my hair, on a boat called the *Bellissimo*. Would you like to hear about that?'

'Um . . . yes, of course,' Bessie says.

But it's a mistake to say yes, because an hour later Paolo's still talking. Once he's off, he barely stops for breath.

Fred, predictably, snaps first.

'I've just worked out why you're here,' he barks. 'It's because none of your owners can stand your endless chuntering drivel-talk. You never shut up, do you?'

Bessie shushes Fred, but she might as well not bother because Paolo doesn't even seem to hear Fred. He just keeps talking.

'My own daddy liked to play in a field of grass,' he's saying another hour later. 'But not any kind of grass. He didn't like straggly grass. Or long grass. Or wispy grass. He liked short grass—'

'So he could be seen over the top of it,' Mitch interrupts.

Or tries to. Because we soon learn that you can't successfully interrupt Paolo. And when the *Bellissimo* boat story and the daddy-in-the-grass story is over, Paolo just carries on.

Mitch eventually screams for mercy and covers his ears. Even Vicky, endlessly patient with all dogs, starts drumming her fingers irritably at the low-level *bark-bark-bark* coming from Paolo's cell.

But nothing deters Paolo. He just keeps going. It's

astonishing. Only when Sloppy Steve takes him down to T-bone for some jabs and a general medical check-up does he pause, and even then only because his tail gets caught in the door on the way out.

'I think I'm going to actually die if he doesn't shut up,' Bessie says, once he's gone. 'Can you die of being talked to, Mitch?'

'I reckon you can,' Mitch groans, his face screwed up in pain. 'What's the matter with him?'

'I've got a feeling he spent most of his time alone as a puppy,' Bessie says. 'Poor thing. He must have started talking to himself out of desperation and, well, never stopped.'

We're all looking at the door, dreading the sound of Paolo returning, when an elderly woman tiptoes into the kennel on flat blue shoes.

She's frail, with thinning white hair. After trudging up the staircases to the third floor, she looks out of breath.

'Er, excuse me,' she says in a delicate voice, 'I'm hoping to view a dog.'

'What? Oh, hello!' Vicky gives her a smile. 'I'm sorry. I was lost in thought there. I didn't hear you come in.'

'Oh, don't worry, dear. People often say that,' the woman replies, taking an extra couple of breaths. 'I'm a quiet person. My name's Gladys, by the way. I'm looking for . . .' She frowns. 'Erm. I can't quite remember his name . . .'

Mitch, Bessie and I cautiously look up.

Gladys reaches into a beige handbag and slowly draws out her reading glasses. She takes her time positioning them around her large ears.

'There, that's better. Now, where was I?'

'You were going to check which dog you wanted to see,' Vicky says with a smile.

'Oh, yes. That's right. And now I've got my glasses on I can see very well which one it is. It's that lifeless one – the one in the corner.'

Vicky blinks a few times. 'You mean . . . you mean Fred?'

'Fred. Yes. That's the one,' Gladys says firmly. 'He's been here forever, hasn't he? A bit of an old duffer. Well, so am I. I'm sure we'll be well matched.'

For a few seconds Vicky doesn't say anything at all. She's in shock. We all are. It's been at least two years since anyone's asked specifically to see Fred.

Recovering fast, Vicky skips across the kennel, grabs the biggest chocolate cake she can find and practically crams it into Gladys's hand.

'Oh, Fred!' she gushes. 'I'm glad you're here about him. Isn't he wonderful? Isn't he an absolute darling?'

'Yes, yes,' Gladys says. 'But even if he's not, I'll probably take him.'

Vicky laughs almost hysterically. She eats a bit of the cake. I'm not sure she even knows she's doing it. 'Right, right,' she laughs. 'Of course. Ha. Ha. Er . . . let me show him to you.'

'That would be nice, dear.'

Fred's heard this whole exchange, but he doesn't move. He's just lying on his side, his big belly splodged across the floor. That's typical of Fred, but this is not a typical situation.

'You need to get up, mate,' Mitch says. 'This is it. This is your chance. Don't blow it.'

Fred stays unmoving. Even when Vicky ruffles his head, saying to Gladys, 'He's just asleep. I'll wake him up and let you two say hello,' Fred refuses to budge.

When Vicky opens his cell, Gladys totters in and bends down to touch Fred's face.

'Oh, he's such an old boy, isn't he?' she says, sounding pleased rather than disappointed. 'I lost my husband recently. He looked a bit like this as well towards the end. Did a lot of sleeping. It's quite comforting, actually, to find a dog who's not constantly on the move.'

'Oh, you're right,' Vicky says, rubbing Fred's ears to get him to at least twitch. 'Come on, Freddy,' she says sweetly. 'Come on, now . . .'

Fred's not asleep, of course. He's faking it. He's wide awake – just not playing ball.

'Fred, stop lying there like an idiot!' Mitch growls.

No response.

'Oh, well, I suppose he'll wake up sooner or later,' Gladys says, not in the least bothered. She adjusts her handbag and prods her glasses more firmly over her eyes. 'I'll wait.'

'I'm sure he'll wake up in a moment,' Vicky says, her smile fixed as she gives Fred a secret dig in the ribs.

'Finding a person who wants to take on an older dog must be difficult for you,' Gladys says. 'Arthritis and vet bills to worry about. Fred in particular's got a lot of expensive health problems to deal with, from what I've read on the website. Luckily, I've inherited a pension from my late husband and I've no one else to spend it on.'

Gladys tells us a lot more about herself while she waits for Fred to respond, but in fact she's just . . . waiting.

Fred, though, is even better at waiting. He does nothing. He won't stir. He won't even look at Gladys.

I shake my head. Fred's had his chances to go home before. Not many, but when I first arrived at Happy Paws I saw him at least turn around and walk up to visitors, greet them with a little wag.

He hasn't done that for years, though.

Bessie's almost in tears, watching him.

All Fred has to do is walk up to Gladys and she's his. You can see that. Probably all he has to do is turn around and look at her *just once*. That's all she's waiting for. Some kind of acknowledgement. Any kind. One tiny little flick of that big rudder-like tail of his . . .

But no.

80

'Fred!' Bessie begs finally. 'For goodness sake!'

'An old codger like me can't be very exciting, I suppose,' Gladys says, talking directly to Fred now as she strokes his face. 'You probably don't want to spend the rest of your days with an oldie like me, do you?' She says it so gently that it sounds like she's asking Fred to take her on instead of the other way around. She's a gift to Fred, we can all see it. She's perfect.

But finally even this patient woman, even Gladys, wavers.

I see the moment when it happens, her smile turning down a little, then a little more and a little more.

Until it's gone.

'Well,' she says several minutes later to Vicky, taking her hand off Fred for the first time, 'not to worry. I think he sees me, all right. He's not really asleep, is he? He's seen me and maybe he just doesn't quite like the look of what he's going to get, that's all.' Gladys forces a smile. 'Which is fair enough. I don't think I'd be much impressed by me if I were a dog, either.'

'No, no,' Vicky says quickly. 'It's not that at all, Gladys. Fred's a fine dog. He just needs a little coaxing. He's been here so long that it's very hard for him to make the effort now.'

'Yes, I can see that,' Gladys says. 'Well, that's all right, dear. Perhaps I'll come back another time, when he's a bit more sociable, and we'll try again.'

But Vicky can see that Gladys doesn't look as if she

81

will come back, and it's all she can do to stop herself crying as, with increasingly quiet assurances that she'll return, Gladys slowly makes her way across the kennel and out of the door.

We listen to her soft footsteps shuffling along the corridor and down the stairs.

After Gladys leaves, Vicky gives Fred a haunted look and, for the first time, he looks right back at her ... and I'm not sure what I'm seeing in his eyes, but it's a kind of despair. You can tell he can't help himself. He can't try any more. He just can't.

And though Vicky is vexed and frustrated, she seems to sense that, too, and a second later she's in his cell giving his big head a hug. Fred doesn't respond, but Vicky holds him anyway – keeps holding him – and afterwards you can see her crying and, when Sloppy Steve returns, to give him credit, he sees that as well and manages to get through the rest of the afternoon without moaning once.

But Paolo doesn't stop moaning. From the moment he's back he's chuntering away. The vet room wasn't quite as sweet-smelling as he expected, apparently.

To be honest, after the sadness of Fred sabotaging his own chance to go home, it's nice at first to hear Paolo's voice gabbling on, covering up what would be an awful silence. But when Vicky leaves at the end of the day, turns off the lights, and *still* Paolo doesn't pause for breath, it's finally me who screams, 'ENOUGH!'

'Well, some people have no manners,' Paolo says, momentarily pausing.

But seconds later he's off again, yapping to the walls now, because no one is listening any more.

'Eeeaaaaaawwwwww!' I hear Mitch cry.

I look across to see him upside down like a bat, standing on his head, covering his ears with his paws.

Paolo yaks on serenely. The monologue is mostly about how beautiful his life in Italy was on the *Bellissimo*, and how beautiful a sight he was personally on its deck, and at some point he murmurs to Bessie, 'Anyway, baby, what do *you* think about my stories?'

But when she doesn't answer it doesn't bother Paolo. He just babbles on and on, and I suppose he stops eventually, but when that point is none of us know, because Mitch has stuffed Binky's pork in his ears and the rest of us are all asleep.

# Chapter Eight

I wake at 7.10 a.m. the next day, and I can't quite believe it.

Because, yes, Paolo is *still* talking.

'Gugugugugugugugugug . . .' I glance up to see Mitch's head deep in his water bowl, trying to drown out the sound.

It's less than an hour later when we get a big surprise.

Claire McCracken – the girl who came here a few days ago – is back.

I'm shocked. Very. I thought her mum and sister had rejected me. Why are they here again?

Claire comes crashing through the door as if she's on fire. She runs straight up to my cell, drops her bag on the floor, hunkers down on her knees and puts a finger to her lips.

'Shush!' she whispers. 'Mum and Rowena don't know I'm here.' Reaching quickly through the bars, she strokes my face. 'Hello, Ralph. Did you think I'd forgotten you?'

She surprises me again by whipping a pad and pencil from her bag and starting a sketch.

Vicky is out visiting another kennel, so Sloppy Steve is in charge.

'What are you doing here?' he growls. 'You need to have a parent with you.'

'That's a Happy Paws rule for *minors*,' Claire tells him, rolling her eyes at me. 'Don't you know your own regulations? I'm not a minor. I'm not a child. I'm eleven. That means I can stroke any dog I like unless there's a sign over their cell telling me not to, such as Bessie's.'

We can see Sloppy Steve mulling this over – he's always been cloudy on Happy Paws rules, mainly because he doesn't care what they are.

Bessie, craning her neck over Claire's shoulder, laughs. 'She's drawing *you*, Ralph.'

'Me?'

'Yes. Good likeness, actually.'

Moments later, raised voices echo outside. I recognise one of them as belonging to Claire's mum. And then Rowena is bashing open the door.

She stands there, panting, her face full of venom.

'Here she is! In the kennel! I told you she'd come in here. I told you, Mummy!'

'Go away, Rowena!' Claire yells, suddenly whipping the sketch around to show me.

I don't know what to expect. Something hideous? Or a cute picture that ignores my facial problems? But Bessie's right. It's a decent likeness. Realistic.

Claire's studying my water bowl now as well, and my chew toys. It's as if she's trying to memorise everything.

'Mummy, Mummy!' Rowena shrieks. 'She's in here! I told you she wouldn't leave him alone! We're supposed to be here looking at *cats*,' she yells at Claire, sticking her tongue out at her. 'They're easier to look after, remember! *Not* a dog. So it's stupid you even being in here. Stupid. Stupid. Stupid!'

Claire shakes her head at me. 'Ignore her. I mean, seriously, a *cat*? What idiot wants a cat?'

Mitch has his head out of his water bowl. Ears flapping, face drenched, he's smiling away. 'Hey, I like this girl. She's even made the Italian Stallion shut up.'

He's right. Paolo, curious about Claire, has briefly stopped talking.

'I've got to go now, Ralph,' Claire mutters to me, tucking her sketchbook and pencil away. 'But,' she thrusts her small hand inside the cell and rubs my coat, 'I've got a plan. It's about me and you.' She taps her sketch. 'This is the first part of the plan.'

And with that she's off, Rowena trailing behind her. The two of them run out of the kennel and along the corridor, arguing.

Mitch is laughing, but puzzled as well. 'What was all that about?'

Bessie grins. 'I reckon that girl's decided you're special, Ralph.'

'Nah, I don't think so,' I mumble.

'Oh, I do,' Bessie says with confidence. 'I think you have an admirer.'

Maybe Bessie is right – Claire really does seem to like me – but her mum and Rowena are obviously after a cat now, so I quickly put any silly thoughts about going home with them out of my head.

And, anyway – somebody please help us! – Paolo's endless drone has started up again.

He's focused exclusively on Bessie now, though. She's steadfastly ignored him ever since the first hour of his arrival, but Paolo doesn't seem to care.

'Oh, yeah, baby, me and you on the town,' he promises her. 'Champagne and city lights. New York, Rome, London, Paris, the two of us stepping out every night, babe. Not that I wouldn't give the other girls a wink, that's only charity. A single encouraging wink from Paolo keeps them happy for days and nights at a stretch. They become crazy over me sometimes, you know. They can hardly stand up for being so excited. All they do is think about me – ma fur, ma coat, ma paws . . .'

Eventually, I hear soft groans from Bessie. Being in the cell next to Paolo, she can't ever tune him out.

Paolo thinks she's sighing because she's falling in love.

'Baby, don't feel so bad. Paolo's beside you. You must hate it, those bars between us . . .'

It's about an hour later, and we're all going quietly insane, when an elderly man comes shuffling into the kennel. He's partially deaf – keeps tapping his hearing aid. Vicky welcomes him in, but all he does is say, 'Sorry . . . What . . . Whose name?'

And then I see the moment it dawns on her. Vicky's eyes light up. She takes the elderly man's arm and leads him straight to Paolo's cell. Paolo is talking away, as ever, but the man can't hear him. He really can't.

'He's perfect for you,' Vicky says.

'Who is?' the man asks.

'Paolo.'

'Pullover? Yes, I am wearing one. It's cold outside.' Vicky smiles.

She introduces him to Paulo. Lost in his own conversation, it takes a while for Paolo to realise anyone is watching him. Even then he doesn't stop talking. He just turns his little sausage body around to face the man, mid-sentence.

'Blah-blah . . . ma beautiful body, blah-blah . . . ma cute brown face . . .'

'Well, he's a perky little chap, isn't he?' the man says. 'Nice breed, too. Pedigree. Not too big, either. He'll fit into my ground-floor flat nicely, he will. I can make him a little dog flap for the garden. Do you think he'd like that?'

'Oh, I'm sure he'd love it to bits,' Vicky says, letting the man stroke Paolo.

Five minutes later Paolo's still yapping away when he realises the man is staring at him. In other words, the man hasn't walked away.

I'm sure this must be something new for Paolo, because his eyes suddenly go all big and dewy and, for a second, his mouth actually snaps shut. 'Well, howdy,' he says, licking the man's hand. 'And who may you be?'

Paolo doesn't get an answer, but that doesn't bother him. He just prattles on. What really shocks him is that, when he next looks up, the man *still* hasn't gone. Not only that, he's smiling.

It's obviously a long time since Paolo saw any kind of smile from an owner, because something amazing happens – he begins jiggling up and down with excitement. And, suddenly, he can't help himself –

he's so excited and happy that in mid-sentence he jumps like a squirrel onto the man's knees, and from there leaps right up onto his shoulder.

'Whoa, hey, he's like a monkey, isn't he?' the man says, grinning away as Paolo tumbles off. 'Like my own personal chimp. Oh, I think I'll have him. If, that is' – the man looks worried now – 'he's not already taken.'

'No, no, he's definitely, absolutely available,' Vicky says, nearly jumping onto the man's shoulder herself with happiness. 'We just have a few forms to fill in over here.'

It all takes a while because the man barely hears a word Vicky says, but when Paolo realises he is about to leave, and has been chosen ahead of us, he lifts his head ever so proudly.

I see a tear of relief from Bessie – which Paolo, of course, misinterprets.

'Oh, baby, no shedding tears over beautiful Paolo. He still be in your dreams, darlin'. He be thinkin' of you, sweet girl! Ciao! Ciao!'

And he's off at last, blowing kisses at us as if he's a film star. Lifting his paw on his way out, he gives us an extended celebrity wave and, between the laughter and tears of relief, we all bark our goodbyes and wish him well.

The elderly man pauses on his way out to button up his jacket. Which gives Paolo a few more seconds to take a long, truly impressive bow, and say, *'Sentirete tutti la mia mancanza, lo so.'* Which an Italian dog we meet on a walk at Grace Park later translates for us as, 'You'll all miss me, I know.'

Which, strangely enough, we do.

# Chapter Nine

Early next morning, while she's sorting out other dogs in Reception, Jens leaves a tiny puppy with us for half an hour. We meet her in the chill room.

She's a chocolate-coloured Labrador. Tulip, her name is, and she's so young that there is nothing – literally nothing – that does not *amaze* her.

She can barely stay still long enough to get a sensible word out. As soon as she's introduced to us she's yipping with delight, scrambling across the floor to get to us.

'Hey, hi, hi, hi, hi, hey,' she greets us. 'Me friendly. I love you. I love you. Oops!' She falls over her own feet.

'Sorry! Hi!' She notices me. 'Your face is funny. What are you? Wait, I know! A *dog*!' She grins. 'What kind of dog? No, don't tell me. I know . . . a *big* dog!'

A ray of sunlight strikes her nose. 'Agh!' she squeals, then, 'Ohhh, it's so *warm*.' A child passes in the corridor outside. 'Hey, a tiny person!' Tulip squeals. 'Is it real? Can I play with it? LET ME JUMP ON IT!'

I can see Mitch mentally taking notes for improving the puppy aspect of his own performance.

'Oh, the freshness of her,' Bessie says to me, smiling and breathing in the scent of Tulip's little body.

Bessie's always like this with young pups. It's obvious how much she would have liked puppies of her own. Now that she's been neutered at Happy Paws she won't ever have that chance so, in a sense, puppies like Tulip, Ravi and Cleo are *her* puppies – or the closest she'll get to having them.

Sitting beside her amid the warm soft furnishings of the chill room, I lick her nose.

'What's that for?' she asks.

'Nothing,' I say.

After an ecstatic time crawling all over us, the sleepy Tulip is taken back to the puppy enclosure by Jens and we're led back to our own cells to get ready for today's visitors.

The kennel post arrives about 9.30 a.m. It includes two letters. There's nothing unusual about that, except that the second letter is addressed to me.

93

'A letter to a dog,' Sloppy Steve mutters. 'Must be a joke.' He's about to throw it in the bin when Vicky whips it away from him.

'To Ralph,' she reads. 'Care of Happy Paws Rescue Home. For the attention of Vicky Masters. Please read out to Ralph.'

Vicky blinks at that last part. Repeats it. 'Please read out to Ralph.'

She looks up at me. All the dogs are at the bars of our cells now, ears pricked forwards. Even Fred is curious.

The letter contains a full-colour sketch of me. I'm surrounded by my bowl and toys exactly as they were when Claire last visited.

There's also a note in a yellow envelope. It's from Claire, and Vicky reads it.

Dear Ralph, I hope you are well.

The picture I sent – do you like it? – is a copy of a much bigger one I drew for my mum. I'm keeping it up on the wall in the kitchen. It's there to persuade her that you are the perfect dog for our family. I already know you are. It's just hard getting Mum and my hopeless, stupid, useless, mean, evil sister Rowena to agree.

I also have bad news, I'm afraid. My mum decided to get a cat from Happy Paws. Rowena picked it out.

It's a fat one with a stupid name – Olivia Darling Sparkle. She hisses all day long. You can tell she hates being with us, which is fine by me. I had nothing to do with Olivia. I never wanted a cat.

All I want is you.

It might take me a while to convince Mum she's made an awful mistake. Rowena's stupid fear of you is not helping. To assist me, I wonder if Vicky could write back to let me know how you feel about cats? Can you bear them? If you can, it might help.

Goodbye for now, Ralph. I hope you are having a nice day, surrounded by your great friends Mitch, Bessie and Fred.

Kindest wishes,

Claire

P.S. Don't give up hope!


Vicky puts down the letter and smiles at me.

'Wow, Ralph,' Mitch says. 'You really do have someone fighting your corner! But Olivia Darling Sparkle . . .' He groans. 'If it came to it, could you really live with her?'

'No chance,' I say.

But I hesitate before I say it, and when Mitch sees that he finds it hilarious.

'You and Olivia by a warm, crackling fire,' he whispers. 'Her whiskers pressed close, cheek to cheek . . .'

'Shut up,' I tell him, embarrassed. 'Anyway, it'll

obviously never happen. It doesn't matter what Claire thinks. You can tell her sister and her mum don't want me.'

'But *she* does,' Bessie says softly through the bars.

I'm not sure what to say to that. I'm squirming a bit, to be honest. And for once I'm glad for Fred's intervention.

'Don't get your hopes up, Ralphy-boy,' he says.

'I'm not,' I say stiffly, turning my head away, and this time all three of them laugh.

To cover my embarrassment, I keep working on my backflip. Or my 'smash-your-face-up technique', as Mitch now calls it. He's right, I suppose. So far the best I've managed is a sort of pathetic cartwheel. It definitely gets me noticed by visitors – they mostly walk away in shock.

I'm still practising that afternoon when Vicky rushes into the kennel. The first thing I notice is how worried she looks. That's not like her.

'Hurry,' she says to Sloppy Steve. 'Get the cell ready. He's on his way up.'

'What?' Steve splutters in panic, dropping his newspaper. 'He's coming *here*?'

'I asked for him, Steve. Persuaded Nora we could handle him.'

'But that's ridiculous!' Steve explodes. 'Why do we always have to take on the most unwanted dogs? He'll be a nightmare. He's an ex-fighting pit bull, Vicky! A bloomin' *pit bull!*'

'He's not,' Vicky snaps back. 'The police have already checked him against the dangerous dogs list. He's big and borderline, that's true, but so what? Pit bulls are loyal, gentle animals when raised properly. You're the last person I should have to tell that. The same rubbish is always spouted about Staffordshire bull terriers. They've got a dangerous reputation, but it's all to do with their owners. I've never met a naturally bad one. And, anyway, he's been treated badly. You can tell. T-bone had to operate to repair some internal injuries.'

Steve folds his arms and turns his head away. 'We can't take on another troublesome dog.'

Until that moment you can tell that Vicky has been trying to persuade him, but now her face hardens. 'You're suggesting the dogs in here, *our* dogs, are a problem, are you, Steve? Is that what you're saying?'

Steve backs off right away then, but even so none of us have ever seen him look so worried about a dog coming into the kennel before. What on earth are we getting?

'Listen to Steve!' Mitch says. 'He sounds like he's about to have a heart attack. Did they close down all the cake shops or something?'

'Whoever this dog is, he sounds as if he's in a bad way,' Bessie murmurs.

'Insane, more like,' Fred growls. 'Probably so crazy he attacked a kennel hand. Definitely shouldn't be in with us.'

'Put him next to Bessie,' Vicky says to Steve, pacing the kennel. 'Yes, that's best. Come on, hop to it.' She's annoyed with Steve now. 'Move Mitch along one cell.'

Outside, there's a sudden flurry of noise: heavy stamping boots.

'Wow, look at Sloppy Steve go!' Mitch cries, watching his old cell being mopped in double-quick time. 'Go for the record, boy! WAAAAAAAA!'

Steve's feet and mop really are a blur. He obviously doesn't want to be caught inside when the new dog arrives. Within seconds he has a bowl of water down, a fresh blanket in place and is *outta there.*

More sounds follow on the stairs and the corridor leading up to the kennel, and I see Vicky take a deep breath. She presses her back against one of the kennel walls. It's as if she's looking for strength.

I've never seen her need to do that before.

Then Charley Hawks appears in the doorway. Charley's the strongest of the kennel hands at Happy Paws. He works in kennel two, but he's sometimes borrowed by Vicky when she needs help with a particularly large dog.

Usually Charley carries the dog in if it's injured.

This time it's too big for that. He's trundling the dog on some kind of trolley. I didn't even know they had trolleys like this at Happy Paws.

Sloppy Steve dives out of the way, and we all cram up against our bars as Charley drags the trolley through the main door.

The dog is covered in one of the light green medical sheets T-bone likes to use after surgery.

'He's still asleep, then,' Sloppy Steve mumbles, hanging back and looking relieved.

'Lucky you, eh?' Vicky says acidly. 'Just lay him down nice and gently,' she says to Charley.

Charley does so, bending his knees low so he can take the weight. We're all craning our necks to see, but it seems to take ages before the sheet's finally removed and Charley's able to tip the dog onto the floor. It's done carefully but the dog still slams with a great *thud* onto the waiting blanket.

'Oh,' Bessie murmurs.

Her jaw drops and so does mine. Because is this really a dog?

Yes, but he's not one like we've ever seen before.

He's huge. I've seen plenty of big dogs before – in the kennels and outside – but this dog is half the size of his cell, and almost as broad. His vast head alone seems to take up a quarter of the floor.

Mitch whistles in disbelief.

Edging as close to the new dog as she can, Bessie

lowers her voice. 'The poor thing. He doesn't look well. See those bruises? What . . . what happened to him?'

'Don't get your sympathy up for this one,' Fred warns her. 'Stay back. He's your worst nightmare. An American pit bull terrier crossed with an even bigger dog.'

'A street dog?' I mutter. 'Is that what he is?'

Fred shakes his head. 'No. A fighting dog. Dog fighting is brutal and illegal, but there's big money to be made in that game. Very big.'

I nod. I've heard rumours about the fight houses. The large-breed dogs in kennel six mutter about them sometimes when our paths cross on walks. But I've never met a dog who was part of that scene.

I back away to the edge of my cell and glance at Vicky. Standing next to Sloppy Steve, she checks her notes, then runs a nervous hand through her hair.

'Well,' she says, blowing out a long-held breath, and addressing everyone in the kennel, 'I ask you to give a warm welcome to' – she pauses and marks the name on the kennel chart – 'to Thor.'

# Chapter Ten

Later that afternoon, Thor finally wakes.

As he gets to his feet he looks more like a mountain rumbling around his cell than a dog, and I don't mind admitting I'm afraid of him. We all are.

We get no greeting from him, either. No wagging tail. He doesn't even make eye contact with us. It's impossible to know what he's thinking.

Vicky spends the last hour of her shift alone in his cell with him, but Thor doesn't respond in any way to her soft words and strokes. He looks really forlorn

– and tired, his legs shaking from time to time – but he's also so huge that we can't help but be nervous of him.

That evening is really weird. Normally we chat once the lights first go off, but not tonight. Thor lies like a great silent hulk in the middle of his cell, and we're too intimidated to talk over him. His black hair glistens in the moonlight.

It's Mitch who's finally brave enough to break the tension.

'Hey, Thor, gotta joke for you,' he says. 'One owner says to another, "My cat's got no nose." "How does it smell?" his friend asks him. "Awful."'

There's no reaction from Thor.

'OK, didn't like that one? Try this,' Mitch says. 'Knock knock. Who's there? Ron. Ron who? Ron a little faster, will you? There's a pit bull after us.'

Again, no reaction.

Mitch sniffs, determined not to be intimidated. 'C'mon. You going to talk to us then?'

'A dog like him isn't a social animal,' Fred mutters. 'If he's from a fighting background, he won't be friendly. He'll just rest up. Once he's got his strength back, he'll probably start stalking his cell, wanting to attack us.'

'It's shameful to make a dog fight another dog for money,' Bessie murmurs. 'I can't believe anyone would make a dog do that. What happens if it won't fight?'

'I don't know,' Fred admits.

'Why don't you ask *me*?'

We all jump. The voice comes from the darkness. Thor's cell.

He's looking right at Fred with eyes that are dark blue and gigantic.

I can't read his expression, but his gaze seems to be like that of a robot, calmly taking us all in. I'm sure if he wanted to he could swallow us all in one easy mouthful.

He hesitates, then says in a voice so deep it resounds through the floor, 'I didn't fight, no matter what you might think. But I admit I was bred for it. Trained for it. And my owner, Ian, kept me for two years, trying to make me do it.'

We take that in. Thor's body is like a huge mound in the darkness, but he's trembling as well. You can see he's frightened.

Bessie looks up. 'It must . . . must have been hard to refuse to fight.'

'It was,' Thor says. 'Ian wasn't happy about that. He didn't like it at all. As a punishment, I was kept isolated.'

'Isolated?' Mitch says. 'You mean you weren't allowed to be with other dogs?'

'No, not since I was a puppy. I was kept caged most of the time. I think Ian hoped . . .' Thor's voice catches slightly. 'Oh, never mind.'

'No, go on,' Bessie says gently, moving closer to him.

Thor's head drops almost to the floor. 'I think he was waiting for me to break. He hoped that by keeping me caged it would increase my antagonism – make me angry, I mean – so that if I ever did get loose I'd come charging out and savage whatever was in front of me.'

The moon slips behind a cloud so for a few seconds we can barely see Thor, only hear his heavy breathing.

'Later, Ian changed his approach,' he says. 'He tried giving me the best of everything. Made a fuss over me. Fed me the best cuts of meat. I didn't know why he was making all that effort until one day I overheard his brother say to him, "You must care for the animal to make it love you. If you do that, a dog will fight. No dog, not one dog in the world, will fight hard for you without love in its heart".' Thor pauses, then adds in a whisper, 'But I understood what Ian was trying to do. I knew him only too well by then. And when I still wouldn't fight he finally shoved me in the boot of his car and dumped me here.'

After Thor finishes his story we're all silent. We just lie quietly in our cells, lost in our own thoughts.

It's about half an hour later that we see Thor shaking in his cell. He's desperately trying to hide it, but he can't. You can tell it's the sheer relief of getting away from his old owner.

As soon as she sees the shaking, Bessie walks right up to the bars separating her from Thor and lays a front paw across his. Thor's own leg is so thick that

Bessie's black and white foot is nothing more than a smudge against it, and he jumps in surprise at the contact. It's obvious that no dog has ever been friendly to him before.

Bessie waits for him to recover from the shock of her touch, then brings her paw back across his again.

Grateful, but confused, Thor simply stares at her. He clearly can't understand why Bessie is being nice to him. Even when we spend the rest of the night telling him our own stories, and those of other dogs, it only puzzles him more, because it makes him realise that he knows nothing about the life of an ordinary dog.

He's missed out on *everything*.

He's deeply ashamed of his fighting background as well. Even though he refused to fight another dog, you can tell he doesn't think he deserves to be amongst us. It takes all of Bessie's encouragement to get him to even lift his eyes to the same level as ours. But as she whispers to him throughout the dark night hours, reassuring him that he's safe now, comforting him and telling him how courageous he was not to fight, finally . . . something amazing happens to Thor.

We watch as he timidly shuffles – as shyly as an abandoned puppy – across to Bessie. When he's as close as he can get, he holds back a moment, then touches muzzles with her through the bars of their cells.

Bessie licks him and eases her nose under his immense jaw. I don't know what she's doing at first, then I realise she's lifting Thor's drooping head up as high as she can.

It's just an act of kindness, but it overwhelms Thor. You can tell it's the first time in his life a dog has shown any tenderness towards him.

I think tears might have sprung to his eyes then, if he'd been the kind of dog to shed tears over himself, but it's obvious Thor isn't that sort.

I'm astonished by what Fred does next as well. I almost miss it. He gives Thor a tiny nod of acknowledgement.

'You've come to the right place,' he mutters. 'I never thought I'd meet another dog with less chance of getting out of here than us lot, but now I've met you, Thor, I think I have. Welcome to the No-Hopers. We were four, but now we're five.'

# Chapter Eleven

From that moment onwards, Thor becomes one of us
– an honorary member of the No-Hopers. Never mind
that he's twice the size of the rest of us, dwarfing even
Fred. Basically, he's just like us.

Unwanted.

Because, let's face it, Happy Paws will have to tell
people that Thor comes from a fighting background,
and no family is going to take a chance on a dog like
that. All of which makes him one of the gang. One
of us.

A definite, proper, No-Hoper.

The next morning, the moment Sloppy Steve arrives, he starts giving Thor evil looks. A few minutes later he's openly muttering about 'scary dogs' and 'can't ever trust a dog like that'.

As soon as she hears the bad-mouthing, Bessie's on Steve like a shot, barking at him through her bars.

'Leave him alone, you!' she growls, raising her hackles. 'It wasn't Thor's fault he had a bad owner. He did the bravest possible thing. He *refused* to fight!'

Sloppy Steve can't understand her, of course, but he sees that Bessie kicks off every time he gazes darkly at Thor, so he stops.

'Nice one, Bessie,' Mitch says, giving Steve a matching growl.

'Yeah,' I say, doing the same and nodding towards Thor.

Thor just stares at us in disbelief. You can see how shocked he is to be defended not just by one dog, but three.

Jens comes in half an hour later and introduces herself to Thor by walking right into his cell. Good for her. And when Vicky arrives, after greeting me, she goes straight to Thor as well and wraps her arms around his back as far as she can.

Scary Nora – Happy Paws' boss – arrives just after lunch. She's come for one of her occasional 'chats' with Vicky. It's not hard to guess which dog today's chat will be about.

Nora's a middle-aged woman with long grey hair, short arms and hard blue eyes. Scary Nora's not her real name, of course. Her real name is Nora Whitehead, but we call her 'Scary' because she's forever shaking her head when she comes into our kennel.

You can't blame her for that. Her job is to get homes for all the dogs as fast as she can. Otherwise the kennels get clogged up, and we can't take in new dogs. That's bad. And us No-Hopers are the worst, because we take up cells all year long. We *never* go home.

Despite their differences, Nora and Vicky are great friends, but Thor's a big problem. How will they advertise him on the website?

'What about "Monster dog. Best killer in town. Guaranteed bloodshed",' Nora says, sighing over a mug of coffee. 'Honestly, Vicky, even you can't convince me on this one. No one will want him.'

'He's a good dog, Nora,' Vicky says firmly. 'I can sense it. I don't think he'd harm a fly.'

'Yeah, yeah, I know, he's a real gentle soul with a heart of pure gold.' Nora grins resignedly, then she's suddenly serious. 'Vicky, I need to tell you something. A change of management's coming two weeks from now – a new head of Happy Paws, Davina Singer. She's replacing me.'

'Replacing you?' I can see how shocked Vicky is. 'But, Nora, you've done such a fantastic job!'

'No, that's not true, actually,' Nora says. 'I've struggled with the finances over the last couple of years. Keep this to yourself, but we're almost bankrupt. I've decided to step down in favour of Davina. I'll help her grasp how things are done around here, then I'm going to put all my efforts into getting more donations. Davina Singer's much more experienced than me when it comes to cost-saving. I think she can turn things around and save Happy Paws. But listen, Vicky, she's planning on changes.'

'What sort of changes?'

'She wants to get more dogs in and out.' Nora hesitates. 'I think she might be relaxing the "Do Not Destroy" policy. Tightening the criteria, at least for the long-term dogs.'

Vicky goes completely still when Nora says that. She takes a long, shuddery breath. 'You think my dogs are in danger? She might put them down?'

Nora wavers before answering. 'I don't know what she's planning, Vicky, but you need to watch your step when she turns up. Davina has a reputation for being ruthless with staff who don't share her "vision". You need to be careful.'

Vicky stares Nora in the eye. 'And will you challenge her if she starts making the wrong decisions?'

'I'm going to pick my battles, that's what I'm going

to do,' Nora answers. 'And you'd better do that as well, Vicky. You've got a reputation already for defending just about any dog that comes in. That might have to change if you want to keep your job.'

When Vicky just stares coldly at her, Nora sighs.

'Vicky, I know how you feel about the dogs here in kennel five. I *know*, all right. They're great dogs, and I'm sure I can defend some of them when Davina comes along, but not *every* dog in kennel five. And as for Thor . . . well, look at him. If he's provoked, goodness knows what he's really like with other dogs.'

Vicky's face crumples. 'I know, but . . .'

'It's not just Thor,' Nora says, more softly. 'We've got to be realistic about Mitch, Fred, Bessie and Ralph as well. People are so shocked when they see poor Ralph that our only hope is that out of *sheer pity* they're prepared to take him on. And that never seems to happen, does it? I'm just saying that there's enormous pressure cost-wise to get rid of the dogs that have been with us the longest. On average, when dogs go home, we get a contribution of £70 from their new owner. That's a lot of money we're losing out on week after week because your long-termers never leave. I've been keeping that pressure off you until now, but once Davina arrives I won't be able to do that any more.'

Vicky looks like she's about to blow her top, but instead her shoulders slump and she sinks down.

'How much more time do you think Davina will give me to find them homes?'

'I don't know.'

'Nora,' Vicky rasps. 'I . . . I can't give up on dogs like Thor and Ralph. I just can't. It's why I work in this place. To give them a fair chance, because no one else will.'

'I know, I know,' Nora says quietly.

'No, listen,' Vicky mumbles between rising tears. 'Listen to me. The reason I came to work at Happy Paws rather than another rescue centre is because of the "Do Not Destroy" policy. It's a basic right to life. We don't put dogs down here. And if we can't find a home for them, we look after them. We never give up on them. Maybe no one else cares about them, or ever will, but *we* do.'

'Vicky, I'm on your side, you know that,' Nora says, reaching for her hand. 'And who knows, maybe Davina Singer will agree with you. Let's see what she has to say.'

After Scary Nora leaves I sit in my cell, tail coiled tightly around my legs, feeling shocked. I've never heard Nora openly discuss getting rid of any of us No-Hopers before, let alone putting us down. Luckily, Mitch and Thor were on walks while Nora was here, so Bessie, Fred and I are the only ones who overheard the conversation.

Fred doesn't react in any way, but Bessie does.

'We'd better perfect that backflip of yours after all, Ralph,' she says shakily, trying to make it seem like a joke, but only sounding more scared because of that.

'Yeah,' I murmur. 'But Bessie . . .'

'What?'

'If it's a choice between who they get rid of, between me and you, I mean, I'll never let them take you, you know that, don't you? I'll bite the leg off anyone who tries to do that.'

Bessie leaps in one bound to the front of her cell and tremblingly licks my muzzle.

We agree not to tell the others what we've heard – what's the point in frightening them? – but I have to admit the whole conversation with Scary Nora makes me deeply anxious.

Strangely enough, though, Nora's question of what Thor is really like with other dogs is answered later that day. Vicky's been looking after a tiny Pekinese puppy for the morning called Zena, keeping her on a lead tied to the desk. Sloppy Steve, being even more sloppy than usual, somehow manages to untie Zena while he's fiddling with her collar.

The next second, Zena's off and running as fast as her little legs will carry her.

Puppy freedom.

And since Zena is no more than three inches wide, she squeezes herself into the nearest cell – which happens to be Thor's.

Sloppy Steve nearly dies when he sees Zena jumping up at Thor's face, yipping and yapping, nipping his tail and shouting, 'Play with me! Play with me!'

But a few moments later, when Vicky returns, she's greeted by a wonderful sight: Zena running around Thor in circles, while Thor is laughing and gently cuffing her around the ears.

Zena leaves us later that day, happy and breathless with play, and after she's gone Bessie stares with fierce warmth at Thor thorough the bars of his cell, and he gives her a little nod back.

'See? Vicky's right,' Bessie whispers to me that afternoon. 'He's the gentlest thing. And he's been treated so badly his whole life. We've got to be good to him, Ralph. If this Davina Singer tries to put him down, we have to stop her.'

'I know,' I say. 'I know.'

But inside I'm wondering just how on earth we'd do that.

# Chapter Twelve

We're still thinking about Davina Singer, and tucking into a mash-up of Binky's foul 'super-scrumptious pork bites', when the post arrives.

Amongst the letters is a yellow envelope.

'It's *her* again,' Bessie murmurs to me. 'Claire.'

Mitch laughs, gives his tail a quick chase and we all wait eagerly for what's inside.

There's a new sketch. It shows Claire with me on a lead, accompanied by Rowena and their mum. 'Notice, no cat anywhere to be seen!' a caption says. 'That's my aim – to find Olivia Darling Sparkle a new home by Xmas.'

Even Sloppy Steve finds that amusing, and gives me a wry look.

The accompanying letter is extremely interesting. At least to me.

Dear Ralph,

I just want you to know what a strange cat Olivia Darling Sparkle is!

The only reason she's still with us is that Mum insists that since we took her we have to make every effort to give her a good home. I understand that, but the truth is that all Olivia does all day is hide away, and if we do go near her she just hisses and scratches. She's not a bit happy here.

Anyway, the most important thing I wanted to tell you is that I'm gradually wearing Mum down. I keep telling her that even if we keep Olivia Darling Sparkle we need to get you out of Happy Paws. We have to! You've been in there too long already.

But she's not convinced. She insists that we can't have a dog and when I ask her why, she says, 'Insurance is expensive and food is expensive, too, and vet bills are worse for dogs than for cats.'

So I decided to check into all of that. What I discovered is that lifetime vet bills for dogs are not much different from those for cats, actually. Plus you can get quite cheap insurance from many companies. I rang around and found lots offering a good bargain.

As far as food goes, I told Mum that you can order good-quality dog food from lots of places, especially if you are prepared to buy in bulk.

And when Mum STILL said no, I pointed out that you are used to mostly dry economy-style food in Happy Paws. That means that, while we would obviously give you treats (and don't worry, I'll sneak you plenty of extra ones!), you would not be expecting the most amazing meals every day. So we can cut back on costs there, too. I also reminded Mum that you are not a very large dog so that will help even more with food bills, and, since you have no hair, we don't need to buy a brush!

I think all of this impressed Mum, although she did start laughing.

Anyway, goodbye for now, Ralph. I will continue to work hard on your behalf, and confidently expect you to be with us by the end of the year.

Love, Claire XXX

'That girl is seriously impressing me,' Mitch says, once Vicky has finished reading. 'Apart from choosing you over me, Ralph, she's got such good judgement. Pity about the dead-loss mum and sister. If Claire's having to look up insurance costs they're obviously not listening.'

'Not yet, maybe,' Bessie muses, 'but you never know . . .' And she gives me a huge smile, which I can't help returning.

The letter makes my spine tingle. I won't allow myself to get my hopes up too much, but I don't want to pretend I'm not excited either, so I do a little semiflip in celebration.

Thor looks surprised. 'You all right, Ralph?' he asks, genuinely concerned.

'I'm fine,' I tell him. 'I'm good.'

And my mood improves even more later that day when a hilarious new dog gets Paolo's old cell. Her name is Krinkle.

'Krinkle Krieger,' she informs us, holding out her paw as if she expects us to kiss it.

She's a black and white spotted Dalmatian who comes from a rich household. Fabulously rich – at least according to Krinkle. Her street accent tells us another story.

'I'm just here while they redecorate the mansion,' she informs us. 'Paint fumes can be terribly dangerous, you know, and my nose is *very* sensitive.'

Lot of dogs make up stories like this. They can't bear the thought that their owners have abandoned them. It's obvious just from looking at her that she's an inner-city dog who's led a hard life, probably being passed from one bad owner to another. But she's got guts and she's proud, and if she wants to make up lies about mansions, that's fine by us because she's funny as well. Paolo's tales of luxury on the *Bellissimo* were obviously real, but Krinkle's made-up stories are much more interesting.

'Oh, did I tell you that I won first prize at Crufts, darlings?' she says within a few hours of arriving.

'And what prize was that?' Bessie asks, who knows a thing or two about dog prizes.

'Oh, best spotted dog, or best . . . waggy dog, I think they called it.' Krinkle waves a paw dismissively. 'I can't remember now. It was such a busy day. Luckily, I had the peace and tranquillity of the mansion to return to later.'

Mitch is loving this. He crosses his front paws. 'Did you have many personal servants, Krinkle?'

'Oh, yes,' she tells him. 'About ten, I think. All Labradors. I can't recall their names. Fluffy. Timmy-wimmy. Things like that.'

'I suppose they all become a blur when there are so many,' Mitch says, smiling.

'Exactly. Every Labrador face is so similar to me, darling, so bland.'

Mitch smiles again, happy to indulge her. 'And did you have your own swimming pool, Krinkle?'

'I did, actually, Mitch, yes,' she says. 'Well, a lake actually. The family lake. We own it, you know. And a racing car. A convertible, of course. Standing on the back seat with the wind flying in your face is *so exciting.*'

To be honest, I could listen to Krinkle all day, but unfortunately she gets moved to kennel two the next afternoon.

Soon after she leaves, Thor says wistfully, 'I've never seen a lake. What does one look like?'

'I can't remember,' I admit.

In fact, when we put our heads together, none of us can clearly remember what a lake looks like.

'We really are the No-Hopers, aren't we?' Fred says. 'We've been here for so long that the only thing any of us can remember is this place.'

Shortly after that, we're all tucking into a snack of Binky's sickening 'yummy bacon bites' when Thor says quietly to me, 'Ralph, you know the mastiff that attacked you in Grace Park all those years ago? Can you describe him to me?'

'It's hard to remember,' I say, shivering at the memory. 'It's all a blur now really, Thor. He was massive. Grey with white spots on his face. One of his ears was missing. That was about the last thing I noticed before he swallowed half my head.'

Thor nods thoughtfully. 'You were only a year old? And you took him on just to protect a puppy you didn't even know?'

'Yeah,' I say, rolling my eyes. 'Dumb or what?'

That same afternoon another letter arrives addressed to the kennel. It's not yellow this time, so none of us take any notice until Vicky says, 'Oh, it's Claire again. No, hold on, it's from her mum – Sandra McCracken.'

'I've been expecting this,' Fred mutters. 'She's obviously found out that Claire is writing to us. She's probably furious. Prepare yourself for the worst, Ralph.'

'Shut up, Fred,' Mitch growls.

Vicky reads the first few lines silently, her lips moving to the words, then stops and stares at me.

I can't understand her expression. Happy? Sad?

To Vicky Masters, she reads.

Hello.

This is Claire's mother.

I've discovered that Claire has been sending you letters about Ralph. I'm sorry about that. You must be busy enough without having to deal with her regular complaints.

I certainly know I am. Every single day Claire talks non-stop about bringing Ralph into our home. She never lets up.

She has also answered every single one of my objections to owning a dog. She's researched food, hygiene, veterinary bills, grooming, even training. Most recently, she handed back her pocket money for the last month. 'For Ralph,' she said. 'For things we need to buy for him when the time comes.'

As you know, Rowena is not keen on the idea of Ralph. She always wanted a cat and, frankly, I thought that would be easier for us. However, Olivia Darling Sparkle isn't settled here at all, despite my best efforts. When I phoned Happy Paws to tell them about her constant hissing and scratching they said something is wrong and they agreed to take her back.

Given that, and Claire's unhappiness and PERSISTENT ENDLESS NAGGING, I have decided to come in and have a second look at Ralph. I don't think I gave him a fair chance when I saw him first time around. I'd like to see him again on the morning of 17th November if possible, with a view to taking him home with us.'

When Vicky finishes reading this last line there is stunned silence in the kennel.

'What?' I half-bark.

I'm not sure I've heard correctly. I can't have heard that last sentence right.

'What . . . what did she say about taking me home? *Did* she? . . .'

And then I hear, 'Oh, oh Ralph,' from Vicky, and

when I look up she's crying. She's crying her eyes out. She can't stop. Even Sloppy Steve and Fred look pleased, and Thor has a grin on his face.

As for Mitch, he's going completely nuts, bouncing off the bars of his cell, laughing and yelling. 'Hey, mate! Hey, result! Claire came through! She came through for you! I knew she would! I *knew* it!'

And when I stare at Bessie, it's even more ridiculous. She's so happy that she's jumping in big leaps round and round, barking over and over. 'At last! Oh, Ralph, Ralph, Ralph, Ralph! Ralphy goes home! Ralphy goes home!'

For a few seconds I'm just standing there, looking at them all going crazy. But then – *sphew* – this weird, incredible feeling starts up inside my body. I don't know what it is, but my skin is tingling, my face is hot and my heart is pumping so hard I think it's going to burst, and suddenly, from nowhere . . . I do the backflip!

I do it! The backward somersault.

I don't even know how it happens, but I do it perfectly, landing on all four feet with a great *WOOF*!

It's only in the barking pandemonium which follows that I spot Vicky brushing the tears roughly from her eyes. She's concentrating on the letter again.

Is she frowning? I'm not sure. She's bringing the letter closer to her face, that's for sure, reading the words intently.

'What's wrong?' Mitch chuffs. 'It can't be the letter.

We heard what Sandra said. She's coming to get you, Ralph. She—'

Vicky's squeezing her eyes shut. When she opens them again she's looking at both me and Mitch. Then she places her left hand over her heart.

'Vic, what is it?' Steve asks, puzzled.

'That wasn't the end of the letter,' she whispers. 'There's more.'

Steve snatches the letter from her, and reads it:

I am, however, not yet sure that I will take Ralph. Claire is besotted with him, but I have to think about the future and I'm still concerned about Ralph's long-term potential health issues. I know Claire will not be happy, but I think I can get her used to the idea of another dog if I have to.

Having said that, she has convinced me that it is a good idea to take on one of the long-term dogs you have. I know those are harder to rehome. I personally think that Mitch could be that dog. He's healthy and, although I know he has an issue with cats, we live in an isolated house deep in the countryside so there are simply no cats around here to chase.

Claire is still a child in the end, so the final decision must be mine. I'm not saying we

won't take Ralph; we may do. I'd just like to have a second look at both dogs and choose the one that feels right.
Best regards,
Sandra McCracken

PS: I won't be bringing Claire with me. She will probably lock herself to the bars of Ralph's cage rather than go home without him, so I have not told her about my visit. In fact, she will be at school. She won't know Rowena and I are at Happy Paws. If we choose Mitch, I'm sure Claire will object at first and throw a tantrum or two, but hopefully she'll eventually resign herself to it.

# Chapter Thirteen

Sloppy Steve is the one who eventually breaks the total silence that follows.

'The morning of 17th November,' he says hoarsely. 'That's tomorrow, Vicky. Vicky?'

It's impossible to tell if Vicky's even heard him. She's standing completely still, her eyes darting between Mitch and me. Her hands are over her mouth and nose, as if she can't quite believe what she's just heard.

I can't believe it, either. Mitch versus me? That's not fair. Every time a visitor turns up at the kennel they're choosing between all of us dogs, I know that, but this is different. This is just him or me. It's not right.

My heart is pounding as I look at Mitch, and he's looking right back at me. And then both of us stare at Fred and Bessie, and none of us have any idea what to say.

The remainder of the day goes quietly. Sloppy Steve leaves at 3.45 p.m. as usual, and at 4.50 p.m., ten minutes early, Vicky closes kennel five. Then she takes off the birthday notice – which today for the first time belongs to Thor – and unbolts all our cell doors. Flings them wide.

'Come here to me,' she says to us.

We walk up to her. We let her gather us in her arms. Even Fred comes out. He never normally reacts to anything, but today he does, and Vicky is so pleased to see it that she hugs him right to her chest.

Thor remains in his cell, not wanting to intrude.

'It's all right,' Bessie says softly to him. 'You're one of us now. We always do this at difficult times. Join us.'

'What do I do?' he asks, standing up.

'You don't do anything. You just . . . *We* just stay here together for a while, that's all.'

Thor uncertainly makes his way into the walkway running down the middle of the kennel. Once he's with us, Vicky slumps down with her back against the bars of Fred's cell and just lets us all crash down around her.

I'm not sure how long we stay like this, letting Vicky stroke us as we nuzzle each other and her. All I know is that I can hardly meet Mitch's eye.

127

Why does it have to be him? If it was Fred, maybe I'd feel better about being picked, because Fred doesn't want to go anyway. But Mitch . . .

Vicky gives all of us a bunch of extra treats that evening – leaving new toys in with me and Mitch – and when she turns off the lights she's so emotional she almost forgets to blow us a kiss.

There's a horrible atmosphere in the kennel after she's gone. I wish there was a puppy in with us. Or Krinkle parading her celebrity-mansion stories. Or even Paolo, droning on about the *Bellissimo*.

But no. There's just us No-Hopers.

Me versus Mitch. We can't do that, can we? Lying awake, the two of us pretend to sleep, but at some point I glance across at him and find he's looking right back at me. He grins, embarrassed to be caught doing it.

'We'll just see who gets taken, eh?' he mutters awkwardly.

'No matter what happens, no hard feelings,' I whisper back. 'Anyway, I'm happy if they choose you, Mitch.'

'I'm happy if they choose you too, mate,' he says.

We're both tongue-tied, not knowing what else to say. Later in the night, I hear Mitch clear his throat. 'Man, I just can't go through with this, Ralph. Not after all the chances I've already thrown away. I'll only mess up, chase after some cat miles from the house. This is stupid.'

'It's OK,' I murmur.

'No, I can't take your place,' Mitch says firmly now. 'If they try to take me, I'll . . . I'll bite one of them.'

'*You will not!*'

It's Bessie's voice this time, cutting through the darkness. 'There'll be nothing silly like that. It'll be fair, boys. That's the important thing. Both of you just be yourselves when they turn up. Let *them* decide. You both deserve a home.'

About an hour later, Mitch says, 'I won't do my Performance tomorrow. I'm not doing any of that rubbish puppy pretending stuff.'

'OK,' I say back. 'And I won't do my backflip – which, as you know, is now *perfected.*' We both laugh at that. 'They can just see us . . . see us as we are,' I mumble.

After a while Fred and Thor fall asleep, but not Mitch, Bessie or me.

The night's a cold one in the kennel. At some point before dawn, Bessie whispers to us, 'The dogs I met before I came to Happy Paws were all in competition with each other for prizes. They mostly took on the character of their owners. Only by sharing this place with you have I understood the true meaning of friendship. You're both so special to me. And do you know something? Even if I could have been in a home all this time, by a nice warm fire, I'd willingly have given that up if it had meant never meeting the two of you.'

Mitch finally dozes off. I listen closely as sleep takes him under its spell.

Then I let all the other sounds of the kennel wash over me. Fred's turning restlessly. Thor is huddled into his blanket, kicking his legs out. I can tell he's dreaming. He's a noisy dreamer, making small cries and growls. Outside, a wintry breeze buffets our window and below the sound of that I can hear Bessie's shallow breaths. Without looking at her, I know from the rhythm that she's not asleep yet. I can smell the dust in her cell as well, and the aroma of a half-eaten treat.

When I glance over at her, she's on her side looking right back at me. Her eyes drink me in, as if she's storing up memories for lonelier times to come. Seeing me blinking at her, she smiles and turns away.

'Goodnight, Ralph,' she says. 'Goodnight, lovely boy.'

Next morning my eyes are sticky with tiredness, but I still haven't slept a wink.

Vicky arrives even before Sloppy Steve and, almost in silence, they work on cleaning the kennel. Then

Steve feeds us. Paying real attention to our breakfast choices for once, he doles out a mix of my favourite duck slices and the fish bites Mitch likes so much – not one Binky product in sight.

Not that I can eat anything. From the moment I'm awake, my stomach is doing lurches. Mitch stands there, mechanically chewing his fish, but I can't even touch my food.

Jens joins us at half past eight, and spends some time in the chill room with Thor. After that she puts on a brew of tea and some music, but she can't relax either. None of us can.

Around nine o'clock Sloppy Steve takes Thor down to see T-bone for some injections and a general check-up.

As it ticks around to opening time, Mitch, normally buzzing, is just sitting on his haunches, quietly waiting. I can hardly look at him.

Ten o'clock comes and goes, and we know it could be any time now.

Hopefully it'll be soon. I can't stand the tension.

The hands on the clock slowly jerk round: 10.30, 11.00. Even Sloppy Steve is restless, getting up to clean the coffee and tea mugs.

Vicky barely makes a sound. Teasing out the curls in her hair, she checks a chart, files a few admission forms.

Finally, at 11.35, Sandra and Rowena arrive.

My heart is beating so fast that I can't feel the separate thuds when they open the door.

While Sandra goes straight up to greet Vicky, Rowena ignores me and walks up to Mitch's cell. Bundled up in a brown puffa jacket, she kneels down and waves cheerfully to him.

Fair enough. That's who she wants, then. Her allegiance is with Mitch. I expected that. I'm ready for it.

I stand up and go to the middle of my cell. So does Mitch. Vicky is still talking to Sandra in the office. Steve pops in there, offers to make a cup of coffee, but Sandra looks anxious. She shakes her head. Obviously she wants to get this done.

So do I. Let's get it over with. Before my legs collapse.

Sandra comes out of Vicky's office, unbuttoning her coat. Mitch's cell is the closest to the office, so it's natural that she goes over to him first. Rowena is already there, making a fuss of Mitch. She keeps calling him across to her in a sweet voice.

'Well, here he is,' Sandra says with an uncertain smile, getting down to the same level as Mitch's head.

Mitch looks over at me, as if he wants my permission to approach them. I nod and retreat to the back of my cell to show him it's OK.

He trots forward, lets Sandra and Rowena stroke him, but there's no Performance. He just stands there, allowing them to talk to him and ruffle his coat. He doesn't bark.

Bessie is so tense in the cell next to him that she looks like she might snap. I don't feel tense any more, though. Now that Sandra and Rowena are here, my heart rate has slowed. I feel OK watching them. I don't feel jealous of the extra attention Rowena is already giving Mitch. Well, I do, but I'm calm. I made up my mind last night how I was going to handle this moment.

They finish stroking Mitch.

Then both Sandra and Rowena come over to see me.

They stand at the bars of my cell, and Vicky opens my door.

To give her credit, Rowena is pretty good about things. She obviously still finds me hideous, but she doesn't moan or pull any of the faces she did last time. She's well-behaved. Friendly, even. I could almost cry. Why wasn't she like this last time?

'Ralph, Ralph, we're here!' she says. 'We've come to choose!'

I don't walk forward. I just stay where I am at the back of my cell. Then I lie down, turn my head away from them and stare at the wall. I copy the way Fred does it. It's a gesture that never fails to disappoint people, and it starts working fast.

'What's the matter with him, Mummy?' Rowena mutters.

'Come here, Ralph,' Vicky says, puzzled.

I've never let Vicky down before. I've always greeted everyone who bothers to turn up at the kennel. But not this time. There's no way I'm going to compete with Mitch. I just can't do it.

Sandra is confused now as well. She turns to Vicky. 'Is Ralph OK? He seems to be hanging back.'

'This is not like him at all,' Vicky says, coming straight in to my cell. 'Look at me, Ralph.'

I stare at the wall.

Mitch says, 'What's going on, mate? Hey, what are you doing?'

Bessie whispers, 'Ralph, please don't do this . . . Ralph, please . . .'

But I can't put myself ahead of Mitch. I can't take a place Mitch would have got. I know I'd never be able to live with that.

I'm amazed when it's Fred who speaks next.

'Ralph, stop this.' He's hoarse with emotion. I've barely heard any feeling other than bitterness in Fred's voice before, but this isn't bitterness. It's heartfelt. I glance at him from under my ears.

'Ralph, you . . . you get up, right now!' he orders me. 'This is your chance. Your *one* chance. You get to your feet and go over to meet your new family.'

I gaze coolly at him. 'Why should I? *You* never do.'

'I'm different,' Fred growls. 'No one would want me. I'm a waste of space. You're . . . Bessie's right about you. You're a good dog. Don't make me say anything else. Turn around and greet them. Get up!'

I don't. Instead, I close my eyes.

134

'Ralph!' Mitch barks. 'Ralph, what are you doing? You can't play dead like this.' When I don't respond, he says, 'Right, two can play at that game.'

Backing off from the door, he does the same as me – turns away and flops down in his cell.

Sandra laughs. 'Er, this is odd.'

I can see Vicky desperately trying to figure out what's going on. 'Oh, they're just hungry or something,' she says, buying time. 'Give us a few minutes and we'll have them both happy and wagging their tails again . . .'

While Vicky leads Sandra and Rowena back to the office, Sloppy Steve jumps up and hands out a fistful of treats to Mitch and me. We ignore them.

Mitch growls at me, 'If you're not greeting them, I'm not either.'

Sandra keeps looking nervously back at us and glancing at her watch.

'She's getting ready to leave,' Bessie warns us. 'You two had better stop this or neither one of you is going to get a home.'

When we still don't move, Bessie jumps up, suddenly furious with us both. 'Ralph, that lovely girl, Claire, is waiting for you! And as for you, Mitch, you've messed up all your other chances so far, but take this one if it's offered and make it work this time. You're both good dogs, both equally deserving of a home. Now, get on with it! I mean it! I won't say a word to either of you ever again if you don't make an effort.'

135

Her tongue is like a lash, so sharp that we both get to our feet.

I totter reluctantly to my cell door and so does Mitch.

'OK, we'll . . . we'll do this then,' he says, swallowing.

I can't look at him. 'OK,' I say. 'Best of luck.'

'And you,' he murmurs.

Vicky is so relieved to see us on our feet again that she almost yanks Rowena and Sandra back into the main kennel. 'There, there, all fixed now,' she says, taking a deep breath.

I let Sandra and Rowena pet me. I wag my tail. I show both sides of my face, let them know exactly what they're going to get.

'Good boy, Ralph,' Rowena says, the way little kids do, and it makes me smile.

Sandra gazes closely at me, feels my smooth skin where all the fur has fallen out. Manages to sigh and frown at the same time.

What is she thinking?

I don't know.

She heads back across to Mitch, does the same to him. Lets her fingers linger in his thick, wiry hair. Purses her lips.

She asks a few more questions. They're all about Mitch. None about me. Is that a bad sign?

Then she gets together in a quiet part of the kennel with Rowena and they have a private little chat. I see Rowena nodding strongly.

'OK, then,' Sandra says to her. She takes a deep breath. Heads back to Vicky. Not once does she look at me.

'We'll take him,' she says, pointing. 'I mean, we'll take Mitch.'

Mitch's reaction is instant. A snarl, aimed right at Sandra. 'I'm not leaving you in here, mate,' he says to me. 'No way.'

Sandra and Rowena haven't heard the snarl yet. It's still building in his throat.

I say quickly to Mitch, 'It's you they want, not me. I saw it the second they came in. They only said they'd look at me because of Claire. Hey, listen.' I manage a smile. 'They're not going to take me anyway. Go on – don't waste the chance. Wag your tail.'

Thor gives a loud *woof*, and Fred does as well. I can see Mitch needs Bessie's permission, too, and she gives it to him.

'It's OK to go home, Mitch,' she says. 'It is.'

Mitch takes a long look at Bessie, Fred and me. He nods. His snarl fades, is replaced by a licky tongue.

And that's what Rowena and Sandra get.

Rowena approaches Mitch. Tentatively, she bends down and puts her arms around his neck.

Mitch lifts his head and rubs his face into her hands.

Sandra smiles. She looks pleased. 'Can we do the paperwork now?'

'Yes,' Vicky says. 'I have it ready – for both dogs.

So,' she adds, and I can see she's still holding out hope for me, but trying not to show it. 'So then, no cats at home, eh?'

'No, we're cat-free,' Sandra assures her.

'OK, then. If . . . if you're sure.'

The paperwork takes twenty minutes to complete.

'Will we need another home visit to make certain that our house is suitable for a dog?' Sandra asks.

Vicky puts on a smile. 'No, that won't be necessary. I'll just check with the staff who did your visit for Olivia Darling Sparkle. I'm sure it'll be fine.'

So it's fine. The paperwork's all ready and it's all fine. Everything's fine.

Except it's not, of course. Because Mitch is leaving. He's leaving and I can tell, I just know, that it's for good this time. He won't blow it. He'll think of me and stick it out because he knows I'm left here.

Which means this is probably the very last time I'll ever see him.

I can see Bessie is thinking the same thing. Her mouth is wide open with a grief yet to come.

'Thank you,' Sandra says to Vicky.

'Thank *you*,' Vicky manages to say back. I can see she's trying desperately hard not to look at me. She stands up tall. 'Mitch is a great dog,' she says. 'He's a great, great dog. He's fantastic. You're lucky to have him. But also . . . he's lucky to have you, too. Thank you for giving him a home.'

She holds out her hand and shakes with Sandra and Rowena.

'It's been nice to meet you,' Rowena says politely. She seems aware that Vicky is very emotional, which makes her go quiet herself. 'We'll look after Mitch for you,' she promises.

'You do that,' Vicky says.

'Yes, you do that,' murmurs a dog beside me. 'You keep your promise, little girl. You'd better!'

It's Bessie, lying down, tongue out, hardly able to breathe.

Sloppy Steve fetches a lead. Then Mitch is being led out of the kennel.

HE IS BEING LED OUT.

I know it's goodbye. I do. And the truth is that it always happens fast like this, the leaving part. But this time it's Mitch. It's Mitch and it feels so final, and half my heart is there with him, and although I know it's OK, it's fine, this is a good thing happening, I'm so happy for him, I can't quite accept that these are the last glimpses I'll ever have of my best mate.

As he's going through the door, Mitch stops.

'Come on,' Rowena says gently, tugging on his lead, but Mitch stays where he is, gazing over his left shoulder at us.

He tries to give us a wink and a smile; tries, when that fails, to crack a joke, but he can't quite manage it. In the end he settles for raising his head proudly to

139

each of us, to Fred, to Thor, to Bessie and, finally, to me. Then, with one more fierce nod and a low swish of his tail, he's gone.

# Chapter Fourteen

The kennel isn't the same without Mitch.

No more early morning jokes. No more funny stories. No one banging the walls in excitement when ten o'clock comes round. It feels empty.

Bessie and I miss him so much. Even Fred seems more withdrawn than usual. I think he secretly had a soft spot for our Mitch.

And I can't help thinking of Mitch with Claire. Mitch with Claire. Claire with Mitch. I wish him well, but I won't pretend I'm not jealous. I can't help that.

We're distracted from thinking about him on the following Thursday, though, when Thor is transferred to kennel four. It's all part of Vicky's plan to socialise him with as many new dogs as possible. He'll be touring the other kennels for a few days.

That same afternoon, after our Binky's 'mince balls surprise' (which isn't a surprise, just a gooey mess), we get a *real* surprise – a new woman turns up.

Not a visitor.

She strides into the kennel in a wash of hairspray and pointy heels.

'Hello, I'm Davina,' she says in a tough, clipped voice. 'I started this morning.'

Eek. Our tails sink between our legs. The dreaded Mrs Singer. The new boss of Happy Paws.

'Oh, er, hello,' Vicky says, smiling. 'I'm Vicky.'

Davina gives her a cursory handshake. 'You weren't expecting me?'

'I thought you were starting next week.'

'Mmm. I decided to come in today. Get started on cleaning up a few issues. Out with the old, that sort of thing. A memo should have gone around this morning.'

Vicky blinks at her. 'It may have done. I haven't gone through all my paperwork today yet.'

'Mmm . . .' Davina looks unhappy about that, or about *something*. There's a pout to her lips which gives them a downward, wrinkly pinch in the corners. I get the feeling she often has this look on her face – a dissatisfied look.

She's a small woman. Precise. Her neat red shoes take little, mincing steps across the floor. She has fussy hands, too – thin and dainty, as white as soap – and as she talks they keep gliding in front of her like two pale birds until she notices them and brings them down to her waist.

She hasn't even looked at us dogs yet, but she's looking at Vicky all right. Assessing her closely. And Steve.

'You must be Slo—'

Davina almost says 'Sloppy'. Halts herself in time. She's obviously already heard about his reputation. That's not a good sign.

'Steve Grayson,' she says.

'Yes, I am.' He gives her an uncertain smile.

Vicky opens up all the kennel cells for her to greet us. Davina stays outside. Doesn't even approach. That's a bit odd. Isn't she used to dogs?

'This is Ralph, he doesn't like fish, and this is Fred, who hardly likes eating anything,' Vicky says, trying to break the ice between them. 'You know how dogs are,' she laughs. 'All with their own likes and dislikes.'

'That's not really the way to do things if you need to keep costs down, though, is it?' Davina remarks. 'Nice for the dogs to be given a menu to choose from, but they don't run the place, do they?' She flexes her ankles. 'All dogs should be treated the same: same food, same routines. It's cheaper that way. This is a dog charity, not a hotel. The dogs don't order room service, do they?'

She laughs at her own joke.

Vicky attempts a smile, but I can see she's not impressed.

'Take me through the dogs' *characters*,' Davina says, peering warily at Bessie. 'Describe them to me.'

Vicky does. She's a bit gushy, but not too over the top.

'Mmm, so this is Fred,' Davina says, when Vicky gets to him. 'Yes. I've read his notes. Institutionalised. A real problem. And as for this Thor you recklessly took on, well, with that kind of troubled background . . .'

Vicky reddens. I can see she's about to argue, then thinks better of it. Sloppy Steve is cringing behind her. He's obviously terrified of this woman.

'Make way for the new,' Davina says airily. 'That's my philosophy. We really must get more dogs in and out of Happy Paws you know, Vicky. I hear you do a very good job here. Nora's always singing your praises, and I'm sure it's all true. We'll get along just fine. Oh, by the way, I intend to do an assessment of the longer-term dogs this afternoon. Are you OK with that?'

That catches Vicky by surprise. 'What do you mean, "assessment"?'

'I mean exactly that. An assessment. An appraisal. Any dogs that have been in Happy Paws for over a year will be looked at to test their viability.'

'Viability?' Vicky echoes. 'What does that mean?'

Davina narrows her gaze. 'I sense you see me as your enemy here, Vicky.'

'No, I don't,' Vicky answers quickly. 'Not at all.'

'Good, because I love dogs, too,' Davina says. 'That's why I'm here. But did you know that the overall cost per head of dogs at Happy Paws is the highest of any rescue centre in the area? I saw at first hand one dogs' home collapse due to inadequate cost control and, believe me, that's a tragedy I'm not going to let occur here.'

Davina fixes Vicky with a hard look. 'We're a charity, not a retirement community. The average dog stays for thirty-six days before it's rehomed from the other Happy Paws kennels. That's already far too long, but in kennel five the average is almost . . . well, it's more like thirty-six years.' Davina chuckles herself into a snort. 'Unfortunately, the dogs in this kennel are either unwanted, like Ralph, Bessie, Thor and Fred, or they keep coming back, like . . . who was that dog again?'

'Mitch,' Vicky says, really annoyed by the lecture now. 'And he hasn't come back.'

'Yet,' Davina tuts. 'He hasn't come back *yet*. Anyway, three of the long-term dogs are in here. There are others scattered across various kennels. How many again?' She consults notes in her pocket.

'There are eight dogs who've been at Happy Paws for over a year,' Vicky says tightly. 'What does the assessment involve?'

'It will help weed out the ones that should be moved on.'

'Weed out?'

'Yes. Weed out the ones that still have hope from the *real* no-hopers.'

Vicky blinks. 'Did you say no-hopers?'

'Oh! Yes, I did. Sorry.' Davina frowns. 'I'm not sure where that came from. Must have heard it in another kennel. Amusing term. Anyway, if I feel the assessed dogs may still have a chance of finding a home with us, fine. Otherwise, we'll pass them on to our sister rescue sanctuary in Biston. Perhaps a new setting will help. But if they *completely* fail the assessment . . .' Davina trails off.

'Yes?' Vicky says. 'If they fail . . .'

'Well, other action will be necessary, of course.'

'Other action?' Vicky is staying completely calm now. 'If they fail your assessment, they'll be put down, you mean?'

'Only as a last resort,' Davina says stiffly – and leaves the kennel.

The assessment times are phoned through in the next hour. Sloppy Steve writes them up on the board.

Fred first, at 4.00 p.m. Bessie at 4.15 p.m. Me last, at 4.30 p.m.

'One straight after the other,' Sloppy Steve mutters. 'She's not wasting any time, is she?'

'No, she isn't.' Vicky shakes her head. 'She has a definite agenda. I doubt it'll make any difference what I or anyone else says. Nora gave her the case files on all the dogs weeks ago. I'm worried, Steve.'

'What are you going to do?'

'Nothing yet. If I get into an argument with her, she might exclude me from the assessments. I'm not risking that. Anyway,' Vicky blows out a long breath, 'I can't blame her for wanting to get more dogs out of Happy Paws and into homes, can I? The trouble is, if Ralph, Bessie, Fred and Thor aren't with *me*, who's going to look after them?' She drops her head a moment. 'No. I'll give Davina a chance. Nora was always tough but fair. Maybe this woman will be, too.' Vicky gazes around at all of us, her face haunted. 'I've failed them, haven't I, Steve? I should have been able to get them into homes before now.'

'Don't be stupid,' Steve replies in mid-cake bite. 'Vic, no one could have done more for these dogs than you have. No one.'

Vicky shakes her head. 'No, I've failed them. And now it's come to this: a prissy woman who doesn't even seem comfortable with dogs will decide their fate.'

Steve is silent for a few seconds. 'They'll be OK, Vic,' he says, touching her arm. 'I'm sure they will.'

But *will* we? I doubt it. I glance at Bessie. We're both

afraid. She tries to smile at me, and can't. Fred is a rock in the corner, unmoving. He doesn't even look up at the assessment times.

'It's all starting in half an hour,' I mutter to Bessie, just to say *anything*, break the awful silence. 'You're before me.'

'Beauty before age, eh?' she replies, a shudder in her voice.

I try to laugh. 'Am I really older than you?'

'Yes, by a month, and you know it.'

'What's going on, Miss Bessie?'

The question comes in a high-pitched voice from a puppy called Jimbo. He's only about nine weeks old – a grey whippet, too young to remember much about how he ended up here. Jimbo doesn't understand much of anything, really, but he's friendly enough. He's been bouncing around in the cell next to Bessie for a day or so, chasing his toys.

'We're having an assessment to decide how many extra biscuits we get to eat on our birthdays,' I tell him.

Fred laughs darkly.

'That sounds brilliant!' Jimbo says. 'What's a birthday?'

Bessie gently tells him the truth about what's going on.

'And will *you* be OK, Miss Bessie?' he asks, really worried now.

'I'll be just fine,' she tells him. 'And if I'm not, that's

nothing to bother you anyway. Now eat your snack.'

'But I can't,' Jimbo says.

'Why not?'

'Because I'm not hungry.'

I grin. Right this second, I'm glad Jimbo is here to distract us. 'You'd better eat it or Sloppy Steve will eat it for you,' I tell him.

'Will he?' Jimbo shoves a springy little paw over his bowl.

'You guard that bowl with your life,' I say, winking at him. 'It's not just cakes Sloppy Steve likes. He'll eat anything.'

Fred is called in for his assessment shortly after. He's in there with Vicky for twenty minutes. It's been so long since he even tried to help Vicky find him a home that I dread to think how his assessment will go.

Fred looks bad when he comes back, but says nothing. Vicky returns him to his cell, and when I study her face she's *grey*. Sloppy Steve asks her what happened and she just shakes her head and puts a lead on Bessie.

I manage a quick bark of 'good luck', then she's gone.

She's back less than ten minutes later, looking nervous.

But there's no chance for me to ask what's been decided with her before I'm whisked away.

149

Vicky leads me from the kennel and down the winding metal staircases to Happy Paws' ground floor.

I'm shaking.

'Don't worry, it'll be over my dead body that she gets rid of you,' Vicky mutters, bending down to caress my ears.

What's been decided for Fred and Bessie? I try to work it out from Vicky's face, but can't. Her skin is white, her mouth set in a grim line.

'Something bad's going on, isn't it?' I bark. 'I can tell.'

But there's no time to bark any more because I'm being tugged into an office. I've only seen this office once before, when I first came to Happy Paws.

It's a big office that used to be Scary Nora's.

Nora is sitting there now, behind a big desk, but she doesn't look that scary these days – not compared to the person sitting beside her. The woman who, though smaller, seems to take up all the space in the room.

'Ah, yes,' Davina says, checking her pad. 'Of course. I've been waiting for this one. Ralph.'

# Chapter Fifteen

Davina cleans her round, metal-rimmed glasses.

'This is an unfortunate situation,' she says, scanning her notes. 'A very long-term dog. In fact, apart from Fred, Ralph holds the record, doesn't he? Nearly five years.' She glances down at me. 'A long time to be unwanted, hmm?'

I'm not happy about having that record shoved in my face, and I consider going into a mad, Mitch-type performance to scare her a bit, but I manage not to.

Vicky is shaking. I can feel it through the lead. She's incredibly nervous. It's so unusual to see her like this that I give her hand a lick.

She smiles down at me and marches me up to the desk.

'He's well-behaved, this one,' Scary Nora says quickly to Davina. 'No trouble at all. I personally vouch for him.'

'I'm sure, I'm sure,' Davina says, her long white fingers rippling through her notes. 'It says here he's quite obedient. Knows lots of commands.' She peers down at me over her glasses. 'Sit, Ralph.'

I stay standing. No way am I doing anything she tells me to. Until Vicky gives me a nod, that is. Then I rest back on my haunches and stare at Davina. But as I stare at her I also allow a bit of drool to run off my chin.

Davina gives me a rigid little smile. 'Mm. Over-devotion to a single kennel staff member. Inevitable, I suppose.'

'He's the best dog I've ever known,' Vicky says proudly.

Davina's face is buried in her notes. 'Except he's taking up that valuable kennel space we discussed.' She taps her papers. 'It says here he was in a fight with another dog once.'

'That was a long time ago. It was in defence of a puppy as well. It's how he got to look like this.'

'Circumstances?'

152

Vicky explains about the dog attack. She does it so brilliantly that by the end you'd think I'd personally saved every dog in the world from that mastiff.

I can't tell if Davina is impressed or not, but I jump up and nuzzle Vicky's neck anyway.

Davina gives me a warm smile. For some reason, seeing it makes me shiver right down to my tail.

'Unfortunately, nobody visiting Happy Paws ever cares much what a dog used to be like,' she says. 'They only care what a dog is like *now*, and, for Ralph, that is very unfortunate.'

After making a single, precise mark on a sheet in front of her, Davina slowly puts down her pen and says, 'Well, I think I've made my decision about him.'

'Which is?' Vicky asks.

'You will be informed about that presently,' Davina says. 'Once I've assessed *all* the long-term dogs. I have four to go, so I should be able to let you know by mid-morning tomorrow. Thank you for bringing Ralph in to see me. I can see how devoted you are to him.' She bobs her head at Scary Nora. 'Who am I seeing next?'

'Tonto from kennel one.'

'Oh, yes.'

Vicky, clearly dismissed, stares at Davina a moment longer. Then she turns around and we leave.

Vicky walks me back to kennel five. On the way, she stops at the infirmary, and I'm left for a minute with Toni on Reception. There's a distinct smell of cat in the air and it makes me think of Mitch. At least he avoided the assessments – but what *is* that peculiar scent?

Suddenly I recognise it. Unusually sweet. Only one cat smells like this – Olivia Darling Sparkle.

She's in a large box on a shelf above me, waiting for one of the staff to give her a nail-clip. As I approach, she levels her huge green eyes at me.

I expect insults to follow. Instead she says, 'I've heard about the long-term dog assessments happening today. How did you do?'

'Great,' I tell her. 'They're dedicating the whole of Grace Park to me. They're renaming it Ralphy Meadows. It'll be my new home.'

Olivia Darling Sparkle twitches her whiskers. She actually looks worried for me – which means I must be in the biggest trouble imaginable.

I try to brave it out. 'Why didn't you like it at Claire's house, anyway?'

'Because the real pet-lover in that home so obviously wanted a dog, that's why,' Olivia mutters. Releasing her claws, she licks each in turn with a soft rasp. 'That annoying girl never shut up about you. It was intensely boring. But if I'm absolutely honest, there was one other reason as well.'

'Oh?'

Olivia fidgets with her tail. I've never seen her looking uncomfortable like this.

'Yes . . . well . . . the truth, Ralphy-boy, is that all

those years I was stuck at Happy Paws I was sure I just wanted a cosy retreat by a fireplace. But once I got to Claire's I discovered that wasn't what I wanted at all.'

'Really?'

'Mm, really,' Olivia murmurs, turning to lick her front paws. 'I realised that my place is here. So many kittens are coming into Happy Paws these days. They all need guidance. The staff who run the cattery are always saying how much calmer the place is when I'm there, and, well, I've decided I want to spend the last years of my life here with them, not on my own.'

Olivia stares at me a moment, then checks her already perfectly groomed tail for defects. 'Anyway,' she adds with a grin, 'some kittens come in here with a mistaken notion that you dogs are actually nice. Someone's got to educate them, haven't they?'

Seconds later, Vicky returns. As I'm being led away, Olivia swings her big tail at me in a friendly wave. 'Good luck with your assessment, Ralphy-boy.'

'Thanks,' I mumble. I can see she really means it, and that's good, but boy does it feel weird to be standing there *thanking* Olivia Darling Sparkle.

When we get back to kennel five, Sloppy Steve has duck treats galore piled up in my dish. He's freshly

155

mopped my cell floor as well. All of which makes me feel as if I've already been condemned.

'What happened?' Bessie asks urgently as soon as I'm inside. 'What did they decide?'

'I don't know. What about you?'

But Bessie doesn't know, either. Nothing is going to be revealed until tomorrow.

'Did Davina try to stroke you?' I ask her.

'Of course not. Good job as well. I'd have taken her hand off.'

We both laugh nervously. Then we try to get Fred to tell us what happened during his assessment, but he's pretending to sleep. And he stays that way.

The rest of the day passes normally, except that Vicky stays with us later than usual.

That night is strange, though. Bessie and I are anxious enough, but the real issue is Fred. He's always quiet, but tonight he won't talk at all.

'What's the matter with him, Miss Bessie?' puppy Jimbo asks. 'Is he sick?'

'No,' she explains. 'He's not sick. He's just tired. We're all very tired tonight. You get some sleep now, OK?'

'OK, miss Bessie,' Jimbo says, burying his tiny head in his green-striped blanket. 'I'll try.'

Somehow we get through the night. In the morning, Fred finally stirs but only to take a small drink of water.

Vicky is in early, pacing the floor like a lion, waiting for the assessment results, but she's downstairs when the answers finally come through from Davina by phone.

Sloppy Steve takes the call. We hear muffled words, and Steve makes *oh* and *ah* noises.

At the end of the phone call, Jens, who's been with us all morning as well, cries out in exasperation, 'Well? Come on! What did she say?'

Steve raises a hand. Writes four names on the board: Bessie's, Thor's, Fred's and mine.

Then he starts to add notes against each one. Next to Bessie's name – I cringe, narrowing my eyes, barely able to watch – Steve writes two words:

### No change.

I feel relief. Overwhelming relief. I yelp, almost exploding with happiness. Bessie is OK. She's OK.

Thor is next, and my heart jumps and so does Bessie's as we both watch Steve taking his time over a longer set of words:

### To be reassessed in three months' time.

'Yes!' Bessie shouts. 'Yes! They're giving him a chance!'

Jens and I are whooping, too. So is Jimbo, bouncing

around his cell like a crazy frog. 'Yessssss!' he barks. Then, 'What does reassessed mean?'

'Shush,' Bessie says.

Sloppy Steve brings up his red marker pen again – against my name, this time. Before he writes he pauses to scratch his ear.

'Get on with it!' Bessie growls.

He finally does, but I can't see what Steve writes. He's moved to stand in front of the board. Only Bessie, leaping to stare over his back, can see the words.

She squeals, a huge peal of scattering barks that resound around the kennel.

'Ralph, Ralph, it's OK!' she cries, blinking back her tears.

Steve moves aside and I see it:

## No change.

Bessie's legs are trembling with relief, and I realise mine are, too. I start laughing and so does she. So does Jimbo, though he has no idea why.

Then we see Steve pause against Fred's name.

Fred isn't even looking.

The word *Biston* is scrawled there.

'Biston?' Bessie says, frowning.

'It's OK,' I bark, loud enough for Fred to hear. 'It's another centre, out in the countryside. I don't know what it's like there, but they're definitely not putting Fred down. I've heard Vicky talk about it once or twice.

Smaller place than this, more spread out.'

Fred's head is up now. He nods in that deliberate way he has. I can see the tension leaving his face.

'Hey!' Bessie shouts at him, running up to her bars. 'Don't look happy, then!'

Which brings a small smile out of Fred at last.

Vicky returns moments later. She looks straight at the board. Takes it all in.

'Isn't it brilliant?' Jens yells, hugging her.

Sloppy Steve is happy as well, laughing away. 'There you go, Vic! I told you. That Davina's bark is worse than her bite, eh? She's not so bad.'

Vicky nods, but she looks miserable. 'No, Davina's not so bad,' she admits. 'I had to beg her not to put Thor down, but at least she gave me three months to find him a place. It's just . . .' She falls silent, dragging a hand through her hair.

'What's wrong?' Jens demands.

'Biston's no good, that's what's wrong.' Vicky shakes her head. 'Not for Fred. They don't have the same "Do Not Destroy" policy as us. A dog with his record will get six weeks tops. Then they'll put him down. There's no way Fred will find a home there in six weeks, so Biston's a death sentence for him. They might as well do it now.'

# Chapter Sixteen

The rest of that day is the worst I can remember in all the time I've been at Happy Paws. We're all in a terrible state, trying to absorb the news about Fred. Bessie says a few soothing things to him, but he just stays in his corner with his own thoughts.

I don't blame him. I'd be the same.

Before she leaves at the end of her shift, Vicky gathers Steve and Jens together. 'I've bought us a week from Davina until Fred's transferred. We'll start looking for another centre with a "Do Not Destroy" policy tomorrow.'

That's a ray of hope for Fred, but once Vicky leaves and the darkness settles over us it's hard to remain optimistic.

I don't realise that Jimbo's still awake and worrying about what he's heard until he pipes up in his high voice, 'Mr Fred, what's going on? They're not going to hurt you, are they?'

I don't expect Fred to reply, but he surprises me.

'You go to sleep,' he says. 'It'll be a long day tomorrow.'

'But what's going to happen to you?'

'Shush now,' Bessie murmurs across the kennel. 'You leave Fred alone tonight, Jimbo. He's tired.'

But Jimbo keeps asking questions, and Fred surprises me yet again because he doesn't snap. He just lets Bessie talk Jimbo down and calm him.

Later in the night, Jimbo wakes for about the fifth time, and this time he shuffles over to be as close to Fred as he can. His ears poke though the bars of Fred's cell.

'Mr Fred?'

'Yes? What is it now?'

'Why are you still here at Happy Paws after all this time?' The question sits there unanswered for a long while. Jimbo thinks Fred hasn't heard him. 'What happened to you, Mr Fred? Was it horrible?'

I'm holding my breath for a huge verbal attack on Jimbo. This is incendiary terrain for Fred. Especially tonight of all nights.

And then, very quietly, Fred says, 'There's not much to tell, Jimbo. Another dog replaced me, that's all.'

Jimbo blinks. 'Replaced? What does that mean, Mr Fred?'

Fred turns around to look at him. 'It means I wasn't wanted any more.'

'You weren't wanted? Why not?'

Fred sighs deeply. Finally he whispers, 'I had an owner called Jessica. We used to run a lot together at the park but, as I got older, I couldn't keep up with her. I tried to. I'd puff away, but I'm a big dog and, finally, I couldn't do it any more.'

Jimbo's watching him, wide-eyed. 'I don't understand,' he says.

'She got fed up with me, that's all. Traded me in a for a newer model. A puppy.'

'And you ended up here?'

'Yes. I ended up here.'

Jimbo takes that in. Then he asks, 'But why are you *still* here, Mr Fred?'

There's a long wait this time.

Fred shifts his bulk, spreading his front paws. 'I'm still here because I'm afraid of rejection, Jimbo. It hurt when Jessica dumped me all those years ago. It hurt a lot. I don't . . . I don't want to ever feel like that again.'

I hear Bessie sigh and, as I take a deep breath of my own, Jimbo walks up and licks Fred's muzzle through the bars.

By 7.00 a.m. the next day, long before it's light, Jens, Sloppy Steve and Vicky are already back in the kennel. They're the first day staff to arrive in the building. It's a cold December morning, and the building's heating systems haven't warmed the kennels up yet, so Steve makes mugs of hot steaming tea for the three of them, and Jens stands there stamping her feet to keep warm.

'Right, we need an action plan,' Vicky says, wiping tiredness out of her eyes. 'I know how difficult it's going to be, but somehow we have to find Fred a home in the next week or get him into another rescue centre. I realise you've got the puppies to keep you occupied, Jens, but if you could just ring a few of these places . . .' She hands her a list. 'Bribe them if you have to.'

Jens nods and hugs her.

After she's left, Vicky turns to Steve. 'I'm going to contact every dog rescue organisation, every affiliate of the RSPCA and every shelter that exists in this area if I have to.' She hesitates. 'I know it's a lot to ask—'

'It's OK,' Steve breaks in. 'I'll do my share, Vic. I'll do whatever I can to help.'

Bessie glances at me. Neither of us is sure we believe Steve's words. But from 8.00 a.m., when most of the dog rescues open, he's on the blower.

To give Davina Singer credit, too, she agrees to make Fred top priority in Happy Paws' Reception and rehoming departments. She also makes him both Dog of the Week *and* Dog of the Month on the website. Combined with Vicky putting the word around all the local kennels and rescue centres, it means that over the next three days six people inquire about Fred.

Only one man, however, actually comes in to see him.

He arrives late on a Wednesday morning. Vicky's at lunch – her first real break in days – which means Sloppy Steve's on his own.

He's not used to that. You can see the panic in his eyes when the man introduces himself.

'Name's Malcolm,' he says, thrusting out a hand. 'Where's this old dog of yours, then? Let's have a look at him.'

'Erm, OK. Yeah, fine.' Steve nervously gets up and leads the way to Fred's cell. 'Fred,' he says, 'meet Malcolm. Nice bloke here to see you.'

Fred gives his visitor a tired look, half-raising an ear.

'He's a bit older than I was expecting,' Malcolm grunts, studying Fred though the bars.

'Ah, but old is a good thing where a dog's concerned,' Steve says, giving his best smile.

Malcolm frowns. 'Old is a *good* thing?'

'Absolutely. Younger dogs are loads of hassle. All that guidance and training they need. Worming.

164

Vaccinations. All that *energy*. Very hard work.'

Bessie and I gaze at Steve in amazement. He's delivering Vicky's classic older-dogs-are-best speech – but we've never heard Steve bother with it.

'Do you want some of this, by the way?' he says, placing a slice of ginger cake next to Malcolm. 'We've got loads of treats in the kennel today. It's a special occasion – Bessie's birthday.'

'Er, no thanks,' Malcolm says. 'So you think young dogs are a bad idea?'

'Pfff, I wouldn't have one,' Steve mutters. 'Ripping up your furniture. Chewing your socks. Compared with that, older dogs are a cinch. They're easier to walk and exercise. Quieter and gentler as well.'

Fred's just lying there like a blob during this speech, but he does have one eye open.

'Look at the old fella there,' Steve says, spreading his arms. 'He's gorgeous, isn't he? That big fat hairy belly of his is just, just . . . gorgeous. He's exactly what you're looking for. Dead easy to look after. Stick him by a fire and he'll just lie there vegetating like . . . well, like a vegetable.'

'What, like a tomato or something?'

'Yeah.' Steve's going with it. 'Or a lettuce. Or a carrot, maybe.'

'Actually, I was hoping he had at least enough life in him to go for a walk,' Malcolm grunts, getting down on his knees to scrutinise Fred.

'Oh, he can get about when he wants to, our Fred,' Steve says.

Malcolm looks unconvinced. And he's right to be. Fred rarely even rises to his feet these days, let alone goes for walks – unless Vicky coaxes him.

Making his excuses, Malcolm says he's going to view one more dog in another kennel, and then . . . doesn't come back.

Which is a great pity, though not particularly unexpected.

'But Steve tried,' Bessie says to me. 'I knew you had it in you, Stevie,' she barks at him proudly. 'I just knew you did.'

At the end of that afternoon a chocolate muffin is sitting on the desk next to Steve. Tired from endless phone calls, he glances up. You can see he can't believe it's still there. He's completely forgotten to eat it. It's his favourite flavour, too.

'I've decided I'm going to save it,' he announces, when Jens asks him about it. 'That chocolate muffin will be my reward when Fred gets a home. Until then, not one more cake will pass my lips.'

Jens laughs. 'Steve, if you find Fred a home, I'll buy you a whole cream gâteau every day for the next month.'

I have to admit that Steve stares at that lonely chocolate muffin a lot over the next couple of days, but he doesn't touch it. Instead, he's constantly on the phone. He's already gone way beyond Vicky's original list.

And Vicky, of course, never stops trying for one second. But it's tough out there in the dog rescue world. There's a recession, people can't afford food and vet bills, and dogs are being given up all the time. Every rescue centre is crammed full. A lot of them aren't even taking in young dogs with no problems, let alone a chronic No-Hoper like Fred.

'This is ridiculous!' Vicky yells, slamming down the phone after one especially long pleading call. 'I just want to place a single dog. I must be able to do that! What's the matter with everyone?'

The night before the deadline, Vicky is almost literally pulling her hair out. She, Steve and Jens are sitting in the office long after it gets dark. Jens' face is drawn with tiredness. Steve looks bone weary as well.

'He's Steve Grayson, our deputy kennel manager,' Bessie says to me, 'and he's trying his heart out.'

And she's right. Steve's not as good at dealing with customers as Vicky, but he's been working much harder at it recently, and now he surprises us again.

'I'd take him myself, Vic,' he says hoarsely, 'but I live in a flat that doesn't allow pets, you know that. I just can't.'

'It's all right, Steve,' she says quietly. 'I know you would.'

He would as well. You can see it in his eyes. It's not anything he'd have ever offered to do before, but he does now, and you can tell he really means it.

That's the moment I decide I'll never refer to him ever again as 'Sloppy' Steve.

'Right, time for drastic action,' Vicky says, chewing a nail. 'Davina says she won't postpone Fred's departure for Biston tomorrow, but I've got one more idea. It's not great. I'm not even sure . . .' She shakes her head. 'Oh, but why not try it?' She laughs hollowly, grabs her coat. 'I'll be back before eleven tomorrow when the van comes for Fred. Don't let them take him before then.'

Jens puts her coffee mug down. 'Where are you going?'

Vicky shrugs. 'I dunno. Nowhere, probably. It's a stupid idea. Totally stupid. It'll never work, but we've tried everything else.' She laughs, half-hysterically. 'See you tomorrow.' And with her coat flapping behind her, she's gone.

That leaves Steve to turn off all the lights and lock up. Jens takes his arm as they leave. 'You need a wash, Steve,' she says, not unkindly. 'You're a bit sweaty. You've been working too hard.'

He looks at her and smiles lopsidedly. 'I have, haven't I?'

After they've gone, Bessie looks at me and lifts her nose to the shelf near Steve's red seat.

The chocolate muffin is still there.

That night is the one that Bessie and I have been dreading – Fred's last. We share several terrible hours in the darkness during which Fred says nothing at all. Even Jimbo, who now unfortunately understands exactly what's happening, stays quiet.

Next morning, ten o'clock ticks around and there's still no sign of Vicky.

At 10.47 a.m. the van driver comes to take Fred to Biston.

'You can't delay me, I've got a deadline,' he moans when Steve holds him up.

'No way,' Steve says, folding his arms. 'Not before eleven.'

'Eleven *thirty*, you mean,' Jens lies quickly. 'Vet shots for Fred. Vital. Come on, it won't take long. I'll grab a cuppa with you while we're waiting.' She makes it sound like a good offer and, after a moment, the driver shrugs and lets her lead him to a local café.

Steve carries on biting his fingernails, watching the clock.

At ten past eleven, a woman turns up.

An elderly woman. Very softly spoken, and wearing flat shoes that make her footsteps even quieter than her voice. No one except us dogs with our fine-tuned hearing even notices her until she clears her throat.

'This one's for the chop today, I hear,' she says in a cheery voice.

We've seen her before.

Gladys.

She shuffles up to Fred's cell, bangs on it with her bag.

'Hello there, old-timer. Remember me?' She glances at Steve. 'You might want to open his door, young man. I don't think we know each other. You weren't here last time, were you? Vicky sent me.'

'Vicky?' Steve gawps.

'Yes. Vicky. Can I see Fred?'

'Er, yeah, of course!'

Seconds later, Vicky arrives. She's out of breath. 'Had trouble parking,' she says to Jens.

She looks exhausted. I can tell she hasn't slept. She hasn't even changed. She's still wearing yesterday's clothes.

'What have you been doing?' Jens asks her, taking her coat.

'Looking,' Vicky says, 'for *her*.' She thumbs towards Gladys, who is now outside Fred's cell. 'She mentioned she lived north of Grace Park when she came in before.

170

It's all I had to go on.'

'I don't understand,' Jens whispers. 'How did you find her just based on that?'

'I knocked on doors.'

'How many doors?'

'Dunno.' Vicky shrugs. 'Hundreds, I suppose.'

'In the middle of the night?'

'Had to. I didn't have any choice, did I?' Vicky sniffs, rubbing her chin. 'No one seemed to know who Gladys was. She keeps to herself. People weren't too happy about me waking them up, either. Found her in the end, though, didn't I?'

Jens stares in awe at Vicky. 'Well,' she says, taking her arm. 'You did your part. I guess it's up to Fred now.'

'Yes, it is,' Vicky says, so tired she can hardly stand.

Everyone turns to watch what happens next.

Fred's not looking at us or Gladys. He's not looking at anyone. He's lying on his side, staring blankly at the wall – his usual tactic.

Gladys kneels next to him. She stares at him thoughtfully and puts her handbag down.

'You know something?' she says, speaking directly to Fred. 'I used to be a volunteer here at Happy Paws. I'd walk the dogs every Friday. Socialise them, too. And I was a fosterer for two years. My husband didn't like it much, but he put up with it. Of course, that was a long time ago, and no one here now remembers me.'

Fred lifts his head fractionally, then drops it again.

'It's funny how things get forgotten, isn't it?' Gladys goes on. 'Like me. Like you. There's only this tenacious young lady fighting your corner now, isn't there? Vicky's a bit of a diamond, isn't she? She's a bit mad as well, of course. You wouldn't catch me waking people up in the dead of night.'

Taking a shallow breath, Gladys sighs. 'I don't really like most people all that much, to be honest. But I like dogs, Fred. I do like dogs. And you can sleep at the bottom of my bed if you want, or have downstairs if you like. I don't mind. Food will be basic. No frills. I've only got a pension. It's enough to cover me and your likely vet bills, but only just, mind. I know it's not much of an offer, but . . . well, what do you say?'

And do you know what Fred does?

With all of us watching, he gets up.

He gets up onto his wonky old legs and walks in a creaky totter right up to Gladys. When he reaches her the bars are still between them, but Fred flops his head down as close to where she's kneeling as he can.

Gladys lets out a huge sigh, then reaches forward to stroke Fred. Very gently she does it – just above his eyes. Except for Vicky, I haven't seen Fred let anyone do that to him for years.

The look of surprise on Steve's face is amazing. He just stands there.

Gladys places a wrinkled hand against Fred's flank.

Then, smiling, she says, 'All right, we'll do it then.'

Vicky, watching intently, unhooks a lead from the wall and clips it to Fred. 'He's yours,' she says, swallowing.

'Can I have the red one over there?' Gladys asks, gesturing at where the leads are hooked on the kennel wall. 'I prefer the colour.'

'What do you think, Steve?' Vicky says. 'Can Gladys have the red lead?'

Steve grins. 'I think Gladys can have any lead she wants.'

'Thank you, dear,' Gladys says. Easing up from her knees with a small moan, she takes the red lead Steve clips to Fred's collar and begins to shuffle with him towards the main kennel door.

'But . . . I almost forgot . . . there's paperwork to do,' Steve remembers. 'Isn't there?' He glances worriedly at Vicky. 'Isn't approval needed and everything?'

'It's all right,' Vicky says, her smile so wide now you could drive a car through it. 'I'll do all that stuff later. I've already seen Gladys' home and got the signature I need.'

Bessie and I are staring wide-eyed at all this.

Jimbo is bouncing around his cell. 'Mr Fred, I like your lead! Where are you going?'

Gladys heads towards the end of the kennel. It takes her a while, but Fred moves at about the same speed so they're well matched.

In fact, Fred, looking almost eager, has to wait for her – and he does.

Finally, Gladys reaches the kennel exit and stops. We all take a breath. Why has she stopped? We're afraid to say or do anything. It's like a delicate spell hangs around her and Fred that the least little sound might shatter.

Gladys' handbag is over her shoulder. She unslings it and searches inside. 'Oh, I meant to make a financial contribution to Happy Paws,' she mutters, 'but I forgot to bring any cash with me.'

Vicky steps forward and closes Gladys' bag. 'There's really no need,' she says, kissing her on the left cheek.

'Well, in that case . . .' Gladys shuffles on. Stops again. Tuts. 'Oh, I forgot something else. I've got to get the bus back. It's a while since I tried to get on a bus with a dog. Do the bus drivers still allow it?'

There's a squeal of tension from Bessie.

'Yes, they usually do,' Vicky says. 'As long as Fred's well-behaved. But it depends on the driver. They can refuse if they want. Anyway, I'll take you back in my car.'

'No, no, I wouldn't think of it,' Gladys says. 'I prefer public transport to cars. You can rely on public transport, can't you? Anyway, it's the only way I can travel anywhere with Fred, so we might as well get used to doing it together right from the start, eh?' She chuckles. 'And if the first bus driver doesn't like Fred, we'll wait for the next one, won't we?' She rubs Fred's head. 'Everyone's in such a hurry these days. I don't know why. I'm sure one driver or another will let us on board. I don't think Fred's going to cause a major disturbance on the bus.' Her eyes crinkle. 'Neither of us will.'

She tickles Fred under his chin and Fred drools on her a bit.

'Yes, it's going to be nice living with that,' Gladys says resignedly. 'Well, shall we go, Fred?'

Fred looks at Bessie, Jimbo and me. His ears shoot up and his tail rises.

'Go for it!' Bessie whispers to him, thrusting her face against the bars.

As Fred cranes his neck back to get one more look at us, I tell him, 'Don't chase any cats and get dragged back here, all right?'

'I won't,' he says – and at last we get a smile from him that matches Gladys'.

Next moment, I see Sloppy Steve's arm reaching out for the chocolate muffin. He's been waiting several days to eat it. His fingers fly out almost automatically. He simply can't wait a second longer.

'Oh, is that a cake?' Gladys asks, spotting the muffin. 'I'm a bit peckish, actually. I couldn't . . . I couldn't bother you for a little of it, could I?'

'What?' Steve's face collapses.

'I said I'd like a little of that cake – if it's not too much trouble . . .'

It's hard to describe the look that comes over Steve then. It's a bit like someone chewing a slug.

'Er, no, it's fine, Gladys,' he says in a strangled voice. 'If . . . if you really want it.'

Steve goes to hand the cake to her, but his body won't obey. He actually pulls the cake closer to him. He's hugging it to his belly. 'How much of it do you want?' he whines. 'A half? A quarter?'

'Steve,' Vicky says with strained sweetness, 'give Gladys the *whole* of the cake.'

'But it's massive, Vic,' he says. 'She can't possibly want all of it. She's quite small, and it's so big, and—'

'Actually, I always have a good appetite,' Gladys says. 'I'm quite hungry as well. I was up very early this morning and, what with all the fuss, I haven't had a bite to eat.'

'Really? Haven't you?' Steve squeaks. You can almost see his mind ticking over. 'But this cake is really *old*!' he cries triumphantly. 'You don't want to eat this cake, Gladys. It's days old. It's weeks old. It's *years* old!'

'Well, it looks all right to me,' Gladys says patiently. 'Those kinds of cakes are full of sugar. They last a long time. But if you want it for yourself . . .'

'No, no, not at all,' Steve says and, as if he's just about to die, he turns his head aside, thrusts the cake out and drops it into her hand. 'You have it,' he says, emitting a tiny cry of pain. 'Have all of it. You enjoy it, yeah? Every bit of it.'

'I will,' Gladys says.

And with that, and a quick nod to Vicky and Jens, she walks out of the door with a dog in one hand and a cake in the other.

And that's how Fred went home.

# Chapter Seventeen

'Fred's gone home!'

All day long the words fly around the corridors.

Most of the staff can't quite believe it at first.

'What? You're kidding! Not Fred from five?'

'Yeah, him!'

'Really? Who managed that?'

'That Vicky Masters! She's incredible!'

The jubilation spreads across Happy Paws all day. And no one enjoys hearing the praise for Vicky more than Bessie and me. Vicky's taken so much flak for keeping us No-Hopers. Finally she's getting some recognition. Even Davina Singer is happy to admit that Vicky has the magic touch.

There's a big celebration that lunchtime amongst the kennel staff. All day long we hear laughter coming from everywhere, and the almost impossible-sounding words echoing across the building that it's true, it's true, FRED HAS GONE HOME.

Fresh on the back of Vicky's triumph, Thor returns to us.

He looks good – more confident after meeting the dogs in the other kennels. And instead of everyone muttering about there being no chance of rehoming him, the staff seem much more hopeful.

Because maybe, just maybe, there *is* someone at Happy Paws who can rehome even a dog with his background.

If anyone can do it, Vicky can.

For the next week or so there's a lovely, warm atmosphere in the kennel. Vicky is happy, and Jens buys Steve three birthday-sized chocolate cakes to make up for the muffin he missed out on. As for us dogs, well, we have a good time, too. Vicky lets the four of us spend long periods together in the chill room for the next couple of days. This suits Bessie perfectly as, apart from loving it in there, she's developed a real bond with Jimbo. She's the mother he can't remember – and he's the puppy she never had.

Over the following week or so Bessie teaches Jimbo

everything she knows. He doesn't always listen – is easily distracted – but he tries very hard.

'What if no one likes me, Miss Bessie?' he asks one morning. 'What if I get left here, like, forever and ever?'

'They will like you,' she reassures him. 'If Fred and Mitch can get a home, you can too.'

'Who's Mitch?'

'He was a run-around-all-day sort of guy like you.'

Jimbo beams. 'Was he?'

'Yes. And he had this technique he used on visitors. A puppy act. But you don't need to do that.'

'Why not?'

'Because you *are* a puppy.'

'Oh, yeah.' Jimbo smiles. 'I am, aren't I? What exactly is a puppy, Miss Bessie?'

'It's a young dog, that's all. Now, listen, when you get a visitor, remember that Vicky, Jens or Steve will usually give them a treat to offer you.'

'What kind of treat?'

'I don't know, like a liver bite.'

'Oh, I like liver bites!' Jimbo says, bouncing up and down. 'They don't last long, but they're really tasty. And I like—'

'Yes, yes, I know, you like lots of snacks. Concentrate now,' Bessie says. 'Tell him, Ralph.'

I sigh and do my dad thing. 'OK, the key thing when the customer holds out the snack is not to nip their fingers. That's right, isn't it, Uncle Thor?'

'Oh, yeah,' Thor says, his mouth full of Binky's fatty beef. 'That's very important. No nippy-noodles.'

Jimbo smiles. 'No nippy-noodles. Ha! But Uncle Thor?'

'Mm?'

'What's a customer?'

About a week after that, Jimbo is still with us when Vicky goes on a two-day break. That leaves Steve in charge. In the past that would have worried us, but not any more. However, something unusual happens.

Thor is out for a walk when a man thumps against the kennel door, banging it wide.

Nothing strange there – people often push the door unnecessarily hard – but this man falls flat on his face once he's inside.

'Gruggh,' he moans. When he gets to his feet, he can't stay upright. He wanders all over the kennel, slamming into the walls.

'He's funny!' Jimbo says, jumping around excitedly.

I glance at Bessie. 'He's drunk.'

'He looks harmless, though,' Bessie says warily. 'Keep back from your door, Jimbo.'

'Why?'

'Just do what you're told now.'

The guy does seem harmless. I can smell drink on him, but he's smiling and muttering a song under his breath, and it's pleasant enough.

Vicky's a pro at dealing with this sort of person. We get them coming in to the kennels a lot – drinkers, lonely people or just folk wanting to get out of the winter cold. Dog-lovers, too, who simply come in to have a look at us and go home again.

If Vicky were here, she'd already have a hand on his arm, charming the guy until she could steer him outside.

Steve's not so diplomatic. Instead of quietly leading him out, he shouts, 'Oy, what are you doing in here?'

'What?' the man slurs, tapping the bars of Jimbo's cell. 'I'm just looking, ain't I? What's wrong with that? Nice puppy.'

He reaches out a big arm. Jimbo manages to bounce back before he's grabbed, but Bessie – angry – lunges to the front of her cell to protect him.

She snarls at the man.

And that's when it goes horribly wrong. Because until that second the drunk was moving fairly slowly, but he surprises us all now with how fast he grabs Bessie's collar.

Even when she twists her head and stiffens, he doesn't release her.

'Snarl at me, eh?' He yanks her hard up against the bars. 'Don't you like me, then?'

'Leave her alone!' Jimbo screams. 'Leave her alone!'

I start growling, too, throwing myself at my own bars to draw the man's attention away from Bessie, but it doesn't work. For some reason he won't let go of her.

'Ged off!' he mutters when Steve tries to prise his hand off her collar. 'Ged off me!'

'She can't be handled,' Steve warns him.

'Eh? Keep your hair on. I'm just petting the old girl, ain't I? What's the matter with yer?' He roughly cuffs Bessie's nose. 'There. That's for growling at me.'

Bessie's squirming in the man's hand, but she can't get away from him. I bark non-stop.

'Leave her alone, you idiot!' Steve yells, yanking hard at the drunk's elbow, but the drunk's got such a firm clench on Bessie's collar that he's practically strangling her.

'Miss Bessie!' Miss Bessie!' Jimbo screams.

'Bessie, stop resisting him,' I warn her.

I can see she's trying to do that – trying not to lose her temper – when, inexplicably, the man jabs his fingers right into her nose.

Bessie yelps in agony, springs forward and . . . *bites* him.

It's just a tiny nip on his left ankle, but he reacts as if he's been shot.

'What?' he roars, letting go of her. 'You bit me! You BIT me!'

Bessie retreats, dazed. She's totally shocked by what

she's done. She tries to bark something to me. Can't. Whimpers instead. I watch as she shrinks to the back of her cell, her hind legs collapsing under her.

*Never bite a customer.* How could she do something she's warned the puppies not to do so many times? I can tell she's horrified, can't quite take in what's happened.

'Did you see that?' the drunk bellows at Steve, pulling down his sock. 'Look! That's a huge hole in my leg! That's a gaping wound, that is!' He shows Steve the little puncture mark on his ankle. 'I'll sue you for this! I will!'

When Steve ignores him, the drunk becomes incensed. He grabs Steve by the throat and pushes him up against the bars of Bessie's cell.

'No, Bessie!' I bark, as I see her rushing forward with bared teeth to protect Steve.

That's when something stops everyone.

An unbelievable noise blasts down the kennel from the doorway.

'Rrrruuuuugggghhhhhh . . .'

It's the deepest and most menacing growl I've ever heard.

Thor.

He's back from his walk, led by Peter, one of the newer volunteers.

Sizing up the situation at once, he sweeps in like a storm to defend Bessie. I've never seen anything like the speed of it. Peter can't stop him. He's dragged

184

across the kennel floor as Thor cannonballs into the drunk, knocking him flat on his back.

'No, he didn't hurt me, Thor!' Bessie barks, but it's too late. Thor leaps on the drunk, plants all four feet on his chest and gives him a deep, furious *snarl*.

The drunk screams as Thor clamps his teeth on his left ankle and drags him a few feet away.

As Thor finally lets him go, the drunk scrabbles backwards until he reaches a wall. Blinking at his leg, he looks confused. 'So it was you, then! *You* bit me! Look at him!' he rages at Peter. 'A dog like that, he's massive. What've you even got him in here for?'

Thor stares him coolly down. He's not actually bitten the drunk, I notice. He's just hauled him away from Bessie.

And to confirm that, once she's safely out of the way Steve is easily able to drag Thor off and lock him in his cell – and of course there's no way Steve could ever do that unless Thor allowed him to.

Thor, I realise, isn't out of control at all. He could have dragged the drunk away from Bessie by his arm or his thigh. Instead Thor chose the man's left ankle. The same place Bessie bit him.

Thor's taking the blame for her. He must have seen what happened as he came back from his walk.

'Thor, no, what are you doing?' Bessie whimpers, realising it too. Her paws scratch the floor as she scrabbles towards him.

The drunk gets up. As he staggers out of the kennel, he bellows, 'I'm going to prosecute! That huge dog bit me! Who's in charge here?'

Still shouting, he barges out and down the stairs.

Once he's gone, Steve gathers his wits. 'It's his word against ours,' he says quickly to Peter. 'If we say none of our dogs touched him, they'll believe us.'

'But . . . but I saw Thor grab his leg,' Peter says. 'I can't lie about that.'

'Thor was only defending Bessie and me,' Steve says. 'Come on, Peter, you know what the penalty is for biting someone.'

Peter shakes his head. 'But we're supposed to report it. It's the rules. Anyway, if you're caught lying about it they'll sack you. Do you want to lose your job?'

'Let me worry about that,' Steve says firmly. 'We can't let Thor pay for what that man did, Peter. Don't report it. It'll be a death sentence for Thor. I'll totally back you up. Just stand there and say "no" when anyone questions you. Say the man must have been bitten before he came in. Will you do that?'

Steve and Peter stand there for a long time, with all of us holding our breaths.

Bessie, beginning to recover, turns to Thor. 'Why did you do it?' she murmurs brokenly. 'It was *me* who bit him. I have to take the consequences. Not you. Me, *me* . . .'

'No,' Thor says firmly. 'I can do this one good thing.

This is one fight I'm not ashamed of.'

'Oh, Thor,' Bessie weeps.

Through her tears, we hear sounds outside. Raised voices. It's the drunk man, and he's got someone with him.

Davina.

They enter the kennel together. The man's yelling and showing her his ankle.

'Well?' Davina demands, folding her arms and looking right at Steve. 'What happened?'

Steve makes a point of carefully listening to the ranted accusations of the man, then says, 'I don't know what he's going on about, Davina. He barged into the kennel and barged straight out again. Look how drunk he is.'

Steve sounds convincing, but Davina's not stupid. She glances at Peter. Senses the hesitation in him.

'Tell me which dog it was,' she insists.

Steve's eyes plead with Peter, but Davina's will is stronger.

Peter slumps. Points at Thor.

'I thought so,' Davina says quietly. 'Thank you very much.'

# Chapter Eighteen

Davina leaves with the drunk still shouting in her ear.

As soon as they're gone, Bessie runs up to the bars of her cell separating her from Thor. 'Oh, why did you do that for me?' she pants, licking his muzzle. 'Why?'

'It's OK,' Thor says, lifting his head. 'I wasn't going to let him hurt you.'

'But they'll—'

'I know,' Thor says calmly. 'I understand the penalty. They're going to put me down now, aren't they?'

'Oh Thor, Thor . . .'

'Vicky will deal with this,' I call across. 'If anyone can sort it out, it's her.'

I see Steve already on the phone, leaving an urgent message for Vicky to get back here as fast as she can. I've no idea where she is today. In town? Anywhere she can reach us fast?

'What'll happen to Uncle Thor?' Jimbo calls out, cringing in his cell. 'Will he be OK?'

*No, he won't!* I nearly explode, but manage to stop myself. 'They'll think before they act,' I mutter. 'Take into account that the man was drunk.'

Bessie nods fiercely, but I see she doesn't believe it, and neither do I.

We keep anxiously checking the door whenever there's a noise on the stairs. A dog that bites a customer is normally put down immediately. And Davina Singer isn't the kind of woman to dither.

'I bet she's already talking to T-bone about it,' Bessie silently mouths to me, then suddenly cries out, 'This is my fault, my fault, *my* fault!'

Jens, hearing the news, comes flying into the kennel. 'Where is she, Steve? We need Vicky!'

'I've left her two messages already.'

'I think she's shopping. Keep ringing!' She whips out her own mobile.

Seconds later, the internal phone rings. The kennel phone. Davina's on the other end of the line. I can hear her voice, but not what she's saying. Steve listens, his face slowly morphing into a mask of horror.

'Well?' Jens says when the call ends.

Steve can hardly get his next words out. 'T-bone's making arrangements,' he whispers. 'They're coming to collect Thor in ten minutes.'

As soon as we hear those words, Bessie and I howl.

I wish Thor didn't understand what's going to happen to him, but he does. Fred told him all about biting dogs being put to sleep.

'Bessie, I'm scared, I'm scared!' Jimbo cries out. 'What's going on?'

The one who reassures him, unbelievably, is Thor. 'It's all right. Shush now,' he says. 'Whatever happens, it won't affect you, Jimbo. Bessie and Ralph will stay here. No one's going to hurt you.'

'But . . . but . . .' Jimbo runs wildly round and round, then hides from all the chaos by diving under his blanket.

It's as he's shivering under it that Vicky dashes in.

'What's wrong?' she says to Steve, dropping her shopping bags when she hears us barking. 'Your message didn't make much sense. Tell me quickly.'

'Vic, it's terrible. This drunk man came in . . .'

While Steve's explaining, Vicky rushes across to Bessie's cell and examines her from head to foot to make sure she's OK. She's doing the same with Thor when Steve tells her that Davina's ordered him to be put to sleep.

For a full ten seconds Vicky doesn't move. Her hands stay on Thor's flanks. Then I see her blue eyes narrow into hard slits and her lips press together so tightly that all the colour drains out of them. She stands up. *'When?'*

'Now!' Steve cries. 'Vic, they're coming straight up to get him!'

'Oh, are they? Are they, indeed?' Vicky's eyes smoulder. 'Thor defends Bessie and you from a drunk, and his reward is to be *put down?'* Her voice is so menacing that it sounds like it's coated in blood.

'What are you going to do, Vicky?' Jens says, her hand over her mouth.

You can see the rage building inside Vicky, but her face is scarily calm. She bends down to stroke Thor's ears. 'Does she really think she can sneak your death past me?' she whispers in his ear. 'One of my own dogs . . .' She stabs a finger at Steve. 'Nobody takes him till I get back. You understand? *Nobody!'* And with that she sweeps out of the kennel and down the stairs.

We all wait. Ten minutes go past. Twenty.

Bessie is panting so hard that Steve has to keep refilling her water bowl.

Jimbo remains under his blanket. I'm trying to reassure him, but I'm so nervous that I'm only making him worse.

As for Thor, I've never seen anything like it. He's standing tall in his cell, unbowed. He's like some kind of majestic wolf, nobly awaiting his fate. I've never seen a dog in so much trouble look so composed.

'It's OK, Ralph,' he says, as I pace my cell. 'It's just a different kind of fight, that's all. I'm ready.'

Not long after that we hear the thumping tread of boots marching up the stairs.

'No!' Bessie wails.

Then Vicky bursts in. Her hair is all over the place and there's a rip in one of her shirt sleeves, but she looks serene in a kind of after-the-storm way.

Jens shoots out of her chair. 'Vicky, what did you do?'

We're all up against our bars, listening hard.

'Oh, not much,' Vicky says, pulling a stray hair from her face, Her voice is unnervingly quiet. 'Just checked on a few facts. I asked Davina if she was planning on having anyone stay with Thor to hold him while he got the injection? To gently stroke his neck and face. Anyone he *knows*. When she obviously hadn't thought about that, I asked her if she was intending to be there when it happened; if she had the guts to watch a dog put to sleep on her orders.'

'Oh, Vic,' Jens whispers.

Vicky half-smiles. 'You know what she said to me? That she's the boss, the one who makes the *decisions*. That she's *in charge* and that staff appropriately trained carry out such tasks.'

'What did you do?' Steve asks, the fear growing in his eyes.

'Well, I had no choice, did I?' Vicky says. 'I got the needle from T-bone and stuck it in her.'

We all gape.

'You . . . you didn't, did you?' Jens says.

'Well, not quite,' Vicky admits. 'But I did haul her from that big fancy office of hers into the infirmary to see what happens. All part of her education in Happy Paws and all that. I kicked out the other infirmary personnel and dragged Davina towards the operating table where T-bone keeps the needles. She didn't like that part much.'

Steve sinks into his seat. 'Oh, Vic, what are they going to do now? Make you apologise?'

Vicky laughs loudly. 'No, Steve, they've sacked me, you idiot. I've been given a few minutes to get my personal stuff together. Then security is coming up to make sure I go and never come back.'

'What?' I bark. '*What?*' I jump up, my heart exploding in my chest. 'No, Vicky!' I scrabble across my cell towards her. 'You can't go! You can't leave us!'

Bessie reacts the same way. She yowls. She sounds like she's been hit.

I don't even know what I'm doing. Suddenly I can't see properly. I smash into the bars of my cage, trying to get to Vicky.

'Vicky!' I wail. I know it's pathetic but I can't help myself. She was never meant to go. Not without me. Not if I was still here. 'Not you, Vicky. You can't leave!' I yelp. 'You *can't* leave us!'

Bessie is crying as well, but silently now. I'm banging off the bars of my cell harder than Mitch ever did.

Finally Vicky comes out of whatever state she's in and sees me. With all the energy seeming to fall from her, she unbolts my cell door.

I run into her arms, going mad, barking non-stop.

'Hey, hey, hey, Ralphy,' she says, holding my neck. 'My boy, my Ralphy! It's all right. It's all right.' She bends down, almost crushes me in her arms. 'There are others here to take care of you.' She stares fiercely at Steve and Jens. 'You'll make sure Bessie and Ralph are OK, won't you?'

And they nod. Equally fiercely. They have to. They know she'll never forgive them if they don't.

A security guard comes in. Carl. The tallest security guard we have. Big muscles. Davina's clearly leaving nothing to chance.

'Wait outside,' Vicky tells him loudly. 'I'll be with you in two minutes.'

He exchanges a hard glance with her, then retreats, half-closing the door behind him.

Vicky strides towards Thor's cell.

Seeing where she's going, Carl bundles his way back in. 'Hey, what are you doing?'

Vicky just laughs in his face and unbolts Thor's door.

'You can't do that!' Carl tells her. 'You can't touch anything. You don't even work here any more. You're sacked.'

Vicky ignores him. Within seconds she has a lead on Thor and is walking with him towards the kennel entrance.

Thor can't believe any of this, but he's following her, sticking to her side.

'What's going on?' Jimbo asks. 'Is Vicky taking Thor to T-bone?'

'No,' Bessie tells him, her eyes shining. 'She's not.'

Carl blocks Vicky's way. She halts, glares at him. 'Don't you dare try to stop me.'

He juts out his chin. 'You can't take a dog out of Happy Paws without proper authority.'

Vicky almost laughs. 'You think I'm going to allow anyone to kill a dog of mine whose only crime is to defend a member of staff?'

Carl's never seen anything like the look Vicky gives him.

'It's against the rules,' he says weakly.

When he tries to stop her walking any further, Vicky picks up a departure form from her desk and rapidly fills in three sections. Finishing the last with a flourish of a signature, she levels her gaze back at Carl.

'I'm legally taking this dog, absolving Happy Paws from blame if anything goes wrong,' she tells him. 'Unless, that is, you personally want to be responsible for this dog being put to death, Carl. Is that really what you want on your conscience?'

Carl says nothing, but I can see he's no longer going to stop her.

'One more thing to do,' Vicky murmurs.

She heads straight for me.

'Vicky!' I cry. 'Vicky!'

She smiles at me and, just for a second, my heart leaps because I think she's changed her mind. I think she's going to take me home with her after all.

Thor *and* me? Is it possible?

Vicky fumbles with my door, and suddenly she's coming straight into me, the way I always dreamed she would when we left together, and she holds me in her arms and she's crying.

'It's OK, don't cry,' I tell her, deliriously happy. 'I'm here. I'm ready to go!'

She kneels down and whispers in my ear, 'If it wasn't for Misty . . .' She looks right into my eyes. 'Only Thor's big enough to stand up to a dog like her. I'm so sorry, Ralph. I'd take you home with me right now if I could, but she'd tear you apart.' Her hands are all over me. 'You'll find a home, Ralphy. You will. Even from outside I'll help find you one. I promise.'

I realise she's not taking me away. Of course she isn't. She can't. It was just me being stupid. It was always my dream, that's all – to be with Vicky, running together.

Vicky lets go of me and I lick her fingers as they pull away.

Striding purposefully, Vicky heads towards the door with Thor. She doesn't look at me, and I know it's because she can't bear to.

'You're doing the right thing. I understand!' I bark after her as she goes through the exit. 'It's OK, Vicky! It's OK to take Thor. Get him out of here while you can!'

At the doorway, Vicky stops. She suddenly drops Thor's lead, runs back to me and gives me a final great, crushing hug. Then, picking up the lead again, she runs through the door and is gone.

# Chapter Nineteen

Vicky. Gone. Vicky. Gone. Vicky . . . gone.

I keep saying it to myself for days afterwards. I can't believe it.

Vicky. Gone for good. Gone forever.

It's wonderful that she saved Thor – I'm really happy for him, I don't resent that – but now it's him who has Vicky, isn't it? It isn't me. It's him. It's *him*.

Part of me understands it has to be this way. Vicky's right. I couldn't survive in the same house with a dog as strong and possessive as Misty. But I'd always hoped that . . . well, I suppose I've been waiting for something bad to happen to Misty.

There. I admit it. Like if she died – or did something so terrible that even Vicky had to get rid of her. I'm ashamed of thinking that way, but all this time I've secretly been hoping that if I could only hang on long enough, Misty might vanish somehow and then . . . and then Vicky would be mine.

I've pictured it so many times. Vicky taking me back to her house, me seeing it for the first time, running into the garden – running everywhere.

Because that's the way it was going to be. The way it had to be. *I* was her favourite. She always told me that. 'It's me and you, Ralphy. Always will be. Together we can do anything,' she told me once.

I've lived in hope of that. It's been the hope that Vicky would take me home with her one day that's kept me going at Happy Paws. When my spirits were at their lowest, that's what I thought about. Being rejected all the time by people was horrible, but I could bear it as long as I had Vicky.

But now . . .

A week goes by with no word from her.

Then, on Tuesday morning, Jens reports to Steve that there was some kind of scuffle outside last night.

'Vicky tried to use her old pass to get in to see the dogs,' she tells Steve. 'But she's barred. Her old pass wouldn't work. Apparently she pleaded with the security guard, but he wouldn't let her in.'

'See?' Bessie says, running up to me. 'Vicky is still trying to be with you, Ralph. She is.'

I listen out for her at night after that. Every little noise outside my window wakes me. I listen for hours sometimes, hoping to hear Vicky's voice. Staying awake at night means I'm exhausted during the day, but I'm so miserable I don't care.

It's weeks before I take an interest in anything happening in kennel five again.

When I finally do, I realise that, although Vicky's no longer there for me, some things about life in Happy Paws are better than they were. Vicky's gone, but Fred's gone as well. Unbelievably, he's gone home. And Thor. And my old mate Mitch, too. He hasn't chased after some cat and got himself dragged back here. It looks like he's gone for good this time. I'm sure Claire's got something to do with that. She's the real dog-lover in that house. And Mitch, charmer that he is, has probably won her mum and even the moody Rowena over by now.

Good for Mitch.

But, if I'm honest, other things have changed in a way that's for the better, too. Steve's been promoted to kennel five manager, and he's doing a decent job.

He still has a tendency to flop down in his chair before everything's finished, and he takes an extra nap from time to time, but he's much more conscientious.

He's getting more help from Jens as well. She's found someone to assist her in the puppy enclosure, so she's able to spend more time with Steve and us, which is great.

And I've still got Bessie, of course.

Lovely Bessie.

Over the next couple of weeks other dogs come and go, but as long as Bessie's here I know I can bear it.

Jimbo keeps me grounded as well. The little fella is still with us. He'd have been snapped up long ago except that the puppy enclosure is chock-full and, anyway, he's still too young to go home – which means that Bessie has spent more time with him than with any puppy before. And that means, of course, that she's grown painfully fond of Jimbo.

Being so young and cute, Jimbo also brings more people into the kennel. Today it's a couple. They arrive just after eleven o'clock.

'Er, hi, we're looking for a puppy . . .'

'Ickle puppies!' Bessie and I sing out.

Jimbo joins in, he's so used to it by now. 'I'm an ickle puppy!' he says, doing a strut around his cell.

When they find out he's too young to leave for a few more weeks, the couple head impatiently off to kennel three.

Bessie is sympathising with the disappointed Jimbo when the postman brings a delivery.

It's a letter.

From Vicky.

Before opening it, Steve goes to get Jens and, with her hanging off his shoulder, he reads it out to us.

To all the incredible people and dogs in kennel five, I just want to say how much I miss you all!

The only thing that's got me through this horrible time is Thor. He's a great dog, he really is. His size scares the life out of other owners at the park, but he's doing just fine.

I introduced him to Misty, of course. Misty did her usual – leapt at him, jaws snapping. Most dogs run a mile when she does that. Thor didn't. He just stood there, looking at her.

And Misty sort of . . . stopped.

I can't explain it. I don't know what Thor changed in her, but she just gave him a quick nod, one long sniff, then left him alone. She still rushes other dogs when Thor's not around but, hey, nobody's perfect!

Talking about things that ARE perfect, though, how are my Bessie and Ralph? I tried to get in to see you guys. I even tried bribing the night watchman. Didn't work. So I had a go at sneaking over the wall. I couldn't quite make it.

So here I am, writing instead, and you'll never guess where I'm writing to you from. A school! Yes, I'm at Dallow Road Junior School in Luton, and I'm teaching *kids about DOG CARE! Can you believe that? I thought no one would ever let me work with dogs again after I was dismissed from Happy Paws, but a man I know well from a local dog charity phoned me up when he heard what had happened. He's given me a dream job – teaching kids how wonderful Staffordshire bull terriers and other so-called 'dangerous breeds' can be. It's so rewarding to see the kids come up to stroke the dogs – sometimes scared at first, then realising how friendly they are if handled and treated properly. And because I take them right into the classrooms, I get to have dogs with me all day long. Bliss!*

*Talking of which, I hope Steve and Jens are looking after you guys properly. Steve, are you making sure Ralph gets his duck treat every morning? And Jens – you promised me you'd take Bessie for an extra-long walk at least once a week!*

'Yeah, yeah, I'm doing it!' Jens laughs fondly. 'Go on, keep reading, Steve.'

'All right, all right,' Steve laughs.

*Oh, nearly forgot! I saw Mitch the other day at One Tree Hill Park. He was on a walk with Claire, Sandra and Rowena. You can imagine how he went mad with happiness when I turned up with Thor and Misty. Misty chased him a bit until Thor sat on her, but after that it was cool. We played together for nearly two hours. I noticed Mitch was a bit subdued, but at least he's doing*

OK. Claire says he hasn't left the garden once to chase any cats, so fingers crossed...

Actually, Sandra invited me over for dinner last week at their lovely house in the country. There's so much space there, loads of fields and everything. Mitch seemed a little quiet again, but Claire – well, she's not happy at all. She clearly loves Mitch, but before I left she came to me in tears when her mum was in the kitchen and asked me if Ralph is still at Happy Paws.

Poor thing. She can't get over you, Ralph! Neither can I! I miss you like crazy. And you, Bessie! I bet you're looking as gorgeous as ever. And as for how you are both behaving, I don't even need to ask because you're both always perfect. Be good, you guys, and I'll get in to see you one day soon for sure. I'm working on my tactics right now. And don't think I'm not still working to get you guys out of Happy Paws. I am! In fact, I met a man yesterday, and when I talked to him about Bessie he seemed very, very interested. We shall see!

Ciao for now! ♥

Vicky xxxxxxx

I'm glowing over that letter all day. Vicky's out there, still thinking about Bessie and me. Still trying for us.

'Tell me more about Vicky, lots and lots of stories,' Jimbo says a week later. 'And about Fred and Mitch, Mr Ralph!'

'Your tail's fallen in your food bowl again,' I say to him.

'Oh, yeah.' Jimbo shrugs, moving it. 'Oh, please tell me, Mr Ralph, about . . . about . . . EVERYTHING!'

Bessie sighs. 'He's overexcited again.' She glances across to Jimbo. 'Go to sleep. You haven't had your nap yet.'

'I can't sleep,' he moans. 'It's impossible to sleep. It's *completely* impossible!'

'Why?'

'Because . . . because I want to go outside and play, and because . . . because I want to chase cats, like Mitch did, and I *can't*.'

I groan. I wish I'd never mentioned Mitch's cat-chasing adventures. Jimbo's been obsessed ever since. But a couple of days later I'm glad I told him at least one more colourful Mitch story because Jimbo finally leaves us. He's transferred to the puppy enclosure.

It's a sad day for me, but for Bessie it's awful. She puts a brave face on as Jimbo departs – 'You'll get on great with the other puppies, you'll love it!' But after he leaves she just sits there under her blanket, saying and eating nothing.

With Jimbo gone, Bessie and I become even closer. We don't really know any of the dogs sharing our kennel any more, so we're polite to them but we spend most of our time whispering together.

'It's nearly Christmas, did you know that?' Bessie says to me one day.

'I know. It's only a week away.'

'What do you want as a present?'

'A visit from Vicky,' I say. 'I'll settle for that.'

She laughs. 'Me, too.'

It's the next afternoon that a man enters our kennel.

He's about thirty years old, long-faced, big-nosed, with a beard and sideburns.

Bessie and I watch as he walks up to the desk. Steve's checking medical notes on a Chihuahua fresh in from Assessment.

'Erm, I'm looking for a dog,' the man says.

'A dog?' Steve gets up from his seat. 'Ah, that's a pity. I'm afraid we don't have any left. The last one went yesterday.'

'But . . .' the man looks confused.

'It's OK, mate,' Steve says, grinning. 'Just a little rescue centre joke there. What kind of dog are you looking for? I've got a nice pair of young springers over here, brother and sister, lovely they are.'

'Well, actually,' the man says with a smile, 'I'm looking for *this* dog.' And he points at Bessie.

Bessie nearly drops dead on the spot.

So do I. The only people who ever ask to see Bessie are those passing through the kennel, those who see how pretty she is. No one comes in based on her website page because that makes it clear that she can't be touched. Nobody follows up on a description like that.

Except – this man has. Is he the one Vicky mentioned in her letter?

'Ah, the lovely Bessie!' Steve grins, surprised but chugging into gear. 'Yeah, she's great.'

'May I have a closer look at her?'

'Of course.'

Steve heads across the kennel to open Bessie's cell, but from his expression I can tell how worried he is. He knows that sooner or later the man will want to stroke Bessie and then, if the past's anything to go by, all hell will break loose.

'Stay calm, Bess,' I say quickly. 'This one looks fine.'

'I know, I know,' she mutters. 'Calm, calm, calm.' She briefly closes her eyes.

Steve unbolts her cell door and opens it wide.

Bessie, tail lowered, stands there timidly. Unlike most dogs, she doesn't come forward. She can't. The best she can do is steel herself when visitors want to stroke her. I can see her already beginning to shake – a quiver that runs in a wave from her feet right up through her long elegant black nose.

The man sees it, too. Sizes her up.

'Oh dear, Vicky warned me about this when I met her. That previous owner really did a number on Bessie, didn't she? I've seen it before – over-handled dogs. Terrible.' He glances at Steve. 'Do you think she'll let me approach her?'

207

'Well, if you're careful.'

Steve's right to sound uncertain. Bessie herself never knows quite how she's going to react, and she's worse since the incident with the drunk man.

'It's OK,' I tell her, making eye contact. 'You'll be fine.'

'I know,' she whimpers, lowering her face.

'Keep your hackles down, Bessie. They're raised.'

'Sorry, sorry.'

The man approaches her cautiously. When he enters her cell, I expect him to put his hand forward to touch her immediately. Instead, he surprises me by just sitting down and crossing his legs. He doesn't even go near her.

The relief from Bessie is huge.

'Maybe I can just stay like this for a bit,' the man says to Steve. 'Let her get used to me being in her space. What do you think?'

'I think that's a great idea,' Steve says, beaming. 'Would you like a cup of coffee while you wait?'

'That's very nice of you. I'm Bill, by the way.'

'Nice to meet you, Bill. I'm Steve. How about a choccy biscuit as well?'

Bill nods. 'Sounds good. By the way, whose birthday is it? I saw the notice on the door.'

'Ah, that'll be Ralph,' Steve says, heading to put the kettle on. 'He's the one next to Bessie, looking at you right now.'

'I see,' Bill says, levelling his gaze at me.

'Hi,' I bark, but I'm looking at Bessie. She's still shaking, but she's also curious. It's never happened like this before. Someone *not* touching her; someone leaving her alone.

Pretty soon she gets over her fear enough to manage a small step forward and sniff Bill's shoes.

Steve takes his time making the coffee, and Bill takes his time drinking it. He stays for an hour. A whole hour. Amazing. He passes the time chatting to Steve. He doesn't lay a finger on Bessie.

Bessie's stopped shaking now, but she's still wary of him. She knows he's going to want to touch her at some point. The tension is almost unbearable.

And finally, of course, he does.

'You were prepped for beauty contests, eh?' he says. 'You've got the looks, I can see that. But you don't care to be handled, do you?'

Bill reaches out for Bessie – softly he does it, staying below her chin, non-threatening – and I can see Bessie wince as she feels the weight of his fingers.

A slightly heavier stroke and Bill gets a snarl for his trouble.

'Bessie!' I growl. 'Stop it!'

'Be quiet, Ralph!' she tells me. 'I won't be handled! I won't!'

Bill pulls his hand back. I'm sure he's going to leave now, but he doesn't. He stays where he is.

Bessie is astonished.

'I can see why she's like this,' Bill says conversationally to Steve, as if the snarl never happened. 'I've seen it occasionally in show dogs.'

And with the utmost gentleness his hand approaches Bessie again. The underside of her head.

'Bessie,' I murmur.

'I know, I know!'

And she allows him. She's shaking but she allows him.

Bill rewards Bessie by handling her ever so tenderly. 'I'll not touch you more than this, girl,' he says to her softly. 'But I need to be able to have some comfort if I've got a dog. It'll be just me, no one else bothering you, but I've got to be able to at least do this.'

Bessie nods – at him, at me, at all the other kennel dogs avidly watching – and stays there, not snarling. Bill doesn't move his hand and she doesn't pull away from it. And finally, many minutes later, I see something I've never seen before – at least not when someone has a hand on Bessie. I see her body fractionally relax.

She sighs – and it is a sigh of relief from the bottom of her heart.

'I can do it,' she whispers to me. 'I think . . . I think I can go with this one.'

Bill stays with us another hour or so, and once he can see Bessie is relaxed enough to accompany him, the paperwork is completed.

210

I can't believe what I'm seeing, really, but it *is* happening. Bessie is leaving. She leaves with Bill at just after five o'clock that afternoon.

Before she goes, Steve pushes Vicky's contact details at him. 'I know you met Vicky in the park, but I don't know if she gave you her phone number,' he says. 'I wouldn't bother you, but her address isn't that far from yours and I wonder if you'd just give her a call about Bessie once in a while? She loved that dog. She'll be so happy if you do.'

'I will,' Bill says, tucking the slip of paper into his wallet. 'I'll be more than pleased to.'

'You . . . you don't fancy another, do you?' Steve tries, just as Bill's on his way out. 'Another dog, I mean. I know Ralph's not much to look at, but he's a great dog, and he needs a home too. They've been companions for a long time. I hate to part them.'

My heart nearly bursts. *Yes, yes*, I'm thinking, but not daring to hope. *Please, please* . . .

And I can see the same desperate look in Bessie's eyes.

Will he?

Bill gives me a long solid stare in that quiet way he has. He's a gentle man, I can see that. He's perfect for Bessie.

*And for me. And for me!*

I'm wagging my tail for all it's worth.

'Go on,' I bark, 'take a chance on me, take a chance.'

211

Bill hesitates. 'Look, I'd consider it,' he tells Steve. 'I really would. But I've already got two ditched puppies I've inherited from someone else. One of the reasons I'm taking Bessie is that the website described how good she is with young pups, but I can't take on another adult dog. I just can't.' He looks genuinely regretful.

And I look at Bessie and I smile. What else can I do?

'Puppies,' I whisper to her. 'You're going to have puppies.'

And even though I know it breaks her heart to be led away from me, I can see she's smiling.

# Chapter Twenty

The next few days are the hardest I've ever had to endure. I'm so happy Bessie's gone home at last, but how am I going to survive in this place without her? It was tough enough losing Mitch and Vicky, but Bessie as well?

The whole of the next week is a despondent blur. I hardly sleep or eat. Steve keeps bringing me treats to cheer me up, but I don't even get up for them. I refuse my walks. I just tuck my head under my tail and try to forget everything. Other dogs come and go but I hardly even remember their names.

I wonder if I'm becoming like Fred. Is this what he felt like, stuck here all these years? Am I the new Fred now?

It's at least a week later that my nose picks up a delicious aroma of pork. I wake from a doze to find Steve slipping a bone under my blanket. He sneaks in and sneaks out again.

He's not meant to give the dogs bones. They're mucho expensive. Davina Singer has strict regulations that all the dogs are fed solely on Binky's products these days, but Steve's been bending the rules right from the start, especially for me.

Actually, although he still sags into his red chair a lot, Steve's improved in every way. He's got a new girlfriend as well.

Guess who!

Jens!

This morning she's been helping him bed-in a couple of three-year-old Afghan hound crosses called Miff and Scratch. Except for me, kennel five is all new dogs now.

'Do you think we should ask visitors to contribute towards the cake fund?' Steve asks Jens just after midday.

'You mean ask them to buy the cream cakes you mostly hide from them anyway?' Jens says amiably.

'Well, it's just that they cost a lot,' Steve says, grinning. Then he stares glumly at me. 'Ralph's still barely eating. I'm not sure what to do about it.'

'Don't worry, he'll pick up,' Jens says. 'We just need to be good to him until he gets used to being without the others.'

'We need to get him a home, that's what we need to do,' Steve says.

'Yeah, that too,' Jens agrees. 'And we will. Listen, what about these two new dogs coming in Thursday?' She checks a chart. 'Sisters, Holly and Bobby. One black, the other white. Where shall we put them?'

While Steve's answering that, I give him a little woof of thanks for the bone, and the rest of the morning I take occasional licks of it.

Just after lunch I'm paid a visit by two middle-aged women. They've seen me online and have come in to take a closer look at me. I wag my tail and give them my biggest smile.

'He's an ugly pooch, isn't he?' one says, when she gets up close to me. 'Worse in the flesh than on the website. Whoever took that picture made him look nicer than he is.'

*Thanks*, I think, no longer wagging my tail.

To be honest, I'm so used to these put-downs that they don't bother me much any more. I'm kind of resigned to them – resigned to being here for a long time to come as well. Steve is as enthusiastic about me as he can be when visitors come in but, let's be honest, with this crooked, bashed-in face who's ever going to want me? If Vicky couldn't find me a home, I don't think anyone can.

That afternoon the Dalmatian, Krinkle Krieger, returns after her stay in kennel two. It's disappointing that she hasn't found a home yet, but I'm pleased to see her. Her made-up stories about mansions, family lakes and servants are the funniest I've heard since Mitch left.

'Did I tell you about my long drives into the country, Ralph?' she says that evening after lights out.

'No, I don't believe you did, Krinkle. Did you have your own velvet cushion to sit on?'

'Of course I did,' she says. 'And through the tinted windows I would watch the countryside flow past. Isn't the countryside beautiful, Ralph?'

'I can't remember, Krinkle.'

'Ah, that's a pity. When you get out of here, will you come to my mansion on a visit? We have many guest rooms.'

'I'd like that very much.'

'What kind of ice cream do you like?'

'Oh, any kind. Plain vanilla is fine.'

'Nonsense,' she says. 'I'll order in butterscotch and raspberry especially for you.'

The next day is a bit special. It's almost a real birthday: my fifth anniversary at Happy Paws. Can you believe that? I've been here five whole years.

The staff throw me a little party in the kennel. Staff from other kennels join Jens and Steve as well, and even Scary Nora turns up! She brings me in a whole heap of treats, biscuits and toys and, for old times' sake, I do a quick backflip. Then even more dogs arrive, and I realise Steve has arranged for me to see *all* the old dogs I know who are still at Happy Paws.

'Not a bad somersault,' one dog notes.

It's Ravi, his tongue dangling down – a great dog who should have found a home before now. The good news is that a young family are taking him at the end of the month.

'Hey, Ralph!' he calls out. 'Have you heard any more about Mitch since that letter from Vicky?'

'No,' I tell him. 'No more news.'

'Right,' he says, crestfallen. Then he smiles. 'Anyway, happy fifth, mate! You've got loads of treats, I see. You gonna share them?'

'Definitely.' I nudge a couple towards him with my nose. 'What happened to Jimbo and Cleo, by the way?'

'Cleo went about three weeks ago. A couple took her. They're from Camberwell. Sounds like a nice place. And Jimbo's gone to a family with five children.' He grins. 'Hey, Ralph, you're a bit of a legend, you know. Even amongst the puppies. They've all heard of you now.'

'Thanks to you they have, you mean.'

'No, mate. Nothing to do with me. It's because everyone knows how you got your face injured. They're saying you're the toughest dog that was ever in here.'

'Really?' I frown. 'They never used to think that. How come?'

'Because Thor told them so when he was touring all the kennels,' Ravi explains. 'He let everyone know how you jumped in against a trained fighting dog. He knew the dog that bit you, apparently. His name was Gunner. Thor said he was one of the most ferocious dogs on the fight circuit and that your face is a badge of honour. He says that being as young as you were, and with no help, to voluntarily take on a dog like Gunner was the single bravest thing he's ever heard of.'

I laugh that off, but it explains what's been going on lately – so many Happy Paws dogs, some I've barely met, have been chuffing at me respectfully on my Grace Park walks.

Good old Thor, putting in a word for me. But thinking of him inevitably makes me think of Vicky, and the next hour in the kennel is a sad one as I think about all my old friends. I miss them so much – Bessie and Mitch especially. But even Fred comes into my head a lot. I picture him sometimes, boarding a bus with Gladys, the two of them taking so long to get on that they drive the bus driver crazy.

And then I picture Thor with Vicky again. I keep coming back to that – her playing with him in the park, getting his meals ready, brushing him down.

I can't stop picturing it. I don't think I ever will.

Anyhow, later that afternoon one of my legs is hurting a bit from where I did the backflip, so I tuck it under my flank and have a little rest.

It's at about half past three that a girl comes crashing into the kennel – a young girl. About seven years old. She has dark hair with butterfly grips.

Rowena McCracken.

What's she doing here?

I immediately think, *Oh, no, Mitch is back*, and my heart sinks.

I sort of knew it was too good to last. Mitch just can't resist chasing cats, no matter how far away they are, and he's obviously got himself into trouble again. They're returning him.

Any minute now he'll be hauled back in here with his tail between his legs – which will be great for me, but for Mitch . . .

Sure enough, a few seconds later I hear Scary Nora's voice, and lots of others. They're gathering in the corridor outside the kennel, which is a bit odd, but not that surprising. Mitch is back and they obviously all want to see him. Everyone loved Mitch.

But suddenly there's even more noise and excited chattering and Jens comes bursting in. That's a surprise, too. Normally she's with the puppies in kennel three at this time of day. She must have insisted on being here to settle Mitch back in.

The only question is – where *is* Mitch?

And suddenly I'm scared. I'm scared because Davina Singer is in charge these days, and she hasn't got the soft spot for Mitch that Nora had. After eight messed-up attempts, Mitch was probably on his last try-out for a home before they give up on him.

Maybe Davina's assessing him right now. Maybe she's decided . . . Oh, no, she wouldn't do that, would she?

But it's weird the way people keep racing up the stairs to our kennel. Suddenly the corridor outside is jammed with people, most of whom I rarely see – like Toni Evans from Reception, and even kennel hands like Veronique Cezerac and Gander Swandling, who are normally on evening shift and almost never come into kennel five. What are they doing here in the afternoon? Steve's dashing back and forth, corralling them, trying to keep order, but they're all bubbling with excitement.

'There he is!'

People are pointing at me. And suddenly I'm feeling weird because it's odd to get this kind of attention. I feel even more odd when I spot Scary Nora standing there amongst them all, staring at me with something I've rarely seen on her face before – a smile.

Then Claire McCracken shoots into the kennel.

She almost breaks the door, she's running so hard. With her hair flying everywhere, she shouts, 'Ralph! I'm back!'

'Hi!' I say, really pleased to see her, but still wondering what's going on. Have the whole McCracken family come to bring Mitch back? It certainly makes sense for Claire to be here. She's not the sort of girl who'd be able to let go of any dog until the last minute.

But where's Mitch? Where *is* he?

Claire's kneeling by me now, a huge smile on her face. Then she's tugging at Steve's arm, and telling Jens to 'hurry up', and Jens is laughing and saying 'all right, all right!' and she's unbolting my cell door, and Steve is reaching down to me with the same idiotic smile on his face as Jens and Claire and everyone else in the room.

I can't figure this out at all. It's even more weird when Steve invites Claire to take off my Happy Paws name-tag. She tosses it like a coin at Jens, who pockets it with a wink at her.

'Come on, Ralph!' Claire says, clapping her hands, and suddenly . . . suddenly they're *all* clapping.

And I still don't get it. I still don't understand what's happening. I have no idea at all. All I know is that Steve's gone mad and is handing out cream cakes to everyone in sight!

Then Davina Singer sweeps in, walks up to me and

actually gives my neck a little ruffle. Can you believe that?

'Very good,' she says. 'Very good.'

And all the other dogs in the kennel are barking and woofing, cheering and laughing. They seem to understand, even if I don't, and one of them says, 'Look at his face, he doesn't get it! Ralphy-boy! Ralphy-boy!' And a huge roar of laughter goes up from the rest of the dogs, who all start bashing their bars and kicking their water bowls.

And I *still don't get it*, even when Claire takes my face and rubs her fingers softly all over me and across my neck. But I can smell Mitch on her. She's been touching him recently.

'So where is he?' I bark, digging my paws in. 'This is a lot of fuss for bringing a dog back!' And hearing me say that just makes the other dogs roar with laughter again – which is really annoying, actually.

I turn to let them know what I think of that, but then my head's being whipped around again and Claire's two blue eyes are staring right at me, very close. She's shaking her head and laughing.

They're all laughing!

Then Claire's mother, Sandra, arrives – but still no Mitch – and I cock my head, thinking, *what now?*

'Ralph, I'm here because Mitch is unhappy,' Sandra says. 'Miserable, actually. We couldn't figure out why until we had a word with Vicky. We met her at Peckham

Rye Park and she made a little suggestion. But, anyway, Claire simply would never shut up about you! She would not ever, ever, ever shut up! So finally I thought – and Rowena agreed – oh, all right.'

And I'm thinking, *Er, you thought all right what?*

Then Claire shoves her mum out of the way, grabs my tail and gives it a gentle tug. 'I've got Mitch waiting in the car for you, you idiot. Come on!' she says. 'What are you just standing there for? You know how restless he gets if he's kept waiting!'

And they're all looking at me, and my cell door is open – wide open – and I have no tag, and practically everyone at Happy Paws is there, clapping or smiling or laughing or crying, and finally Steve buries his face in mine and whispers, 'Don't you get it, Ralph? You're going home!'

# Epilogue

Two months after Ralph leaves Happy Paws, Steve is spooning some especially vile Binky's 'super-delicious chicken wobbly-bits' into the bowls of a whole new set of dogs in kennel five when a letter arrives. A letter in a yellow envelope.

Steve opens it, calls Jens across and reads it to her slowly.

Dear Steve and Jens,

Hello! It's me! It's Claire! How are you? I've been thinking how hard it must be for you not to see Ralph, so I thought I'd send you some news about him.

The first thing to tell you is that Ralph, Mitch and I all get to see Bessie a lot. Her new owner, Bill Watson, regularly takes Bessie and the puppies to Peckham Rye Park where we go for walks.

You should have seen what happened when Ralph and Mitch first saw Bessie! At first they couldn't believe it. Then they went totally crazy. They were so happy! It was raining, but we still couldn't separate them for hours.

Now I go to Peckham Rye almost every day so they can spend time together. In fact, next month my mum, Rowena and I are going on holiday with Bessie and her owner. Won't that be great?

Mitch is fine. He loves Peckham Rye Park, especially sniffing around the rose bushes near the Japanese garden where the cats sometimes hang out.

But guess what? Two weeks ago I bumped into . . . you'll never believe it. Vicky!

Yes! She turned up at the same park with Thor and Misty – and the playing started all over again! According to Vicky, Misty used to be a right terror, but not any more. She let me pet her and everything. As for Thor, just the size of him creeps everyone out – and some people don't let their dogs near him – but that's stupid because he's always completely well-behaved.

Back home, of course, Mitch and Ralph play together. Mitch is so happy now that Ralph's with him.

As for Ralph, he can't get enough of the outdoors! We go to the woods, to the river and to the beach. Ralph loves the park, but he loves the sea even more – so we take him whenever I can nag Mum to drive us there. Ralph swims for so long that in the end we have to drag him out in case he drowns!

But there is one problem – with Ralph, I mean. Actually, that's one of the reasons I'm writing to you. Ralph does a strange thing.

He does it everywhere.

He just won't STOP doing it.

So I wanted to ask you about it.

I want you to understand that this thing Ralph does is not a big problem. (And even if he did have a big problem, I'd never let Mum give him back – not that she'd ever do that. She loves him almost as much as I do now, and even Rowena has come round.)

No, this problem isn't that big. I'm only asking because you knew Ralph for a long time, so I wanted to get your advice about it.

You see, once Ralph finishes chasing and playing with Mitch, he will often go off on his own for a little while.

I used to think he just wanted a bit of peace and quiet, but it's not that.

He RUNS.

It's amazing to watch.

He runs in the park. He runs in the garden.

He runs up paths. He runs down them.

He runs in circles.

He runs up hills. He runs along streets.

He runs on the spot.

He runs in straight lines. He runs in zigzags.

He runs EVERYWHERE.

It's not a problem. We love him so much. The last thing we'd ever do is try is to slow him down. But can you please tell me why it is that, all day long, Ralph never stops running?

Yours sincerely,

Claire X

# Author's note

The largest dog welfare charity in the UK and Ireland is Dogs Trust. Every year they care for over 17,000 dogs at their nationwide network of rehoming centres.

What I really love about Dogs Trust is that they do their very best to care deeply for every single dog that comes to them. Their mission isn't just to help abandoned dogs. It's to bring about the day when *all* dogs can enjoy a happy life.

No matter what a dog looks like, whatever that dog's breed or background, Dogs Trust try to find it a loving home. Or – and this is so important – if they can't do that, they take care of the dog anyway.

For life.

They never put a healthy dog down.

Why not go and have a look at their website to see all the great work they do?

www.dogstrust.org.uk

www.dogstrust.ie

Best wishes,

*Cliff McNish*

# the orion star

★ ★ ★